Some Regrets Are Forever

Jane Blythe

Bear Spots Publications
Melbourne Australia

Paperback
ISBN-13: 978-0-6488091-5-9

Cover designed by QDesigns

SAVING RYDER

Christmas Romantic Suspense Series

I'd like to thank everyone who played a part in bringing this story to life. Particularly my mom who is always there to share her thoughts and opinions with me. My awesome cover designer, Amy, who whips up covers for me so quickly and who patiently makes every change I ask for, and there are usually lots of them! And my lovely editor Lisa Edwards, for all their encouragement and for all the hard work they put into polishing my work.

FEBRUARY 3RD

7:12 P.M.

This was it.

The end of the road.

Meadow Smith stepped off the bus and shivered. It was cold out, early February, and although it hadn't snowed in over a week it felt like an icebox out here, but that wasn't why she shivered. The shudder was because her life as she'd known it was gone forever. She was on her own now, and she had no idea how she was going to take care of herself.

The bus driver tooted his horn at her, and she realized that she was still standing in the doorway. Quickly, she moved away. She didn't have a bag with her, she had nothing but a small box in her pocket, and the clothes on her back. The bus ticket had cost her all the money she'd had bar a few measly dollars, and Meadow had no idea what her next move should be.

Where would she stay?

How would she support herself?

What was going to happen to her?

There were no answers to those questions, and with a heavy rock of dreadful trepidation in her stomach, she turned and watched the bus as it drove off down the road.

That bus had been her home for the last couple of days and seeing it leave only intensified those feelings of fear and loneliness. When it disappeared around a corner she shivered again, and tears threatened to spill down her cheeks. Meadow fought them back because in the cold they would feel like tiny blocks of ice against her cold skin, and because she had already cried more tears than anyone should have to in a lifetime.

She straightened her spine, pulled her coat tighter around herself—as much as a shield to the world as a shield against the cold—and started walking. The ticket she had bought—the one that got her as far away from where she had been as she could afford—had brought her to a small town called River's End. Farms surrounded the town, and the bus stop appeared to be at one end of a street that was lined with stores. Most of them were closed since it was after seven, but her eyes immediately zeroed in on light spilling out from one particular shop down toward the other end of the street.

Meadow started walking, and as soon as she did she felt the hairs on the back of her neck stand up.

It felt like someone was watching her.

"You're wrong," she hissed under her breath.

She prayed she was, she really did, but it was hard to believe that this had worked and she was truly free now.

Dark windows stared out at her from the empty shops and houses that lined both sides of the street, and although she couldn't see any faces peeping through them it didn't mean that someone wasn't watching her.

She wondered if that feeling would ever fade. Would there ever be a time where she wasn't constantly looking over her shoulder? Would there ever be a time when she would feel free? Safe? While she hoped that there would be, she wasn't overly optimistic about the possibility. If there was one thing that life had taught her it was that just when you thought you were turning the corner and finally finding something good, you were really about to find yourself in an even worse situation than the one you were leaving.

Was that what would happen to her here in River's End?

Maybe her best option was to just keep moving. Sure she didn't have any money for another bus ticket right now, but maybe there was a way to get a job here, work for a couple of weeks, just long enough to buy another ticket, and then she could move on to somewhere else.

Move and keep on moving.

It would be a lonely life, but perhaps it was her best chance at actually *having* a life.

Sacrifices.

Life was full of them and staying on the move, never remaining in one place for too long, that seemed like it was going to be the sacrifice that life had thrown at her.

She couldn't run forever though, sooner or later she would have to find a place to put down some roots because ...

A scream very nearly tumbled off her lips when she heard a twig snapping behind her.

Someone else was out there.

Meadow spun around, expecting to see someone come running at her, but there was nothing. No one.

Carefully she scanned the road, there were streetlights and fairy lights decorating the trees, but anyone could be hiding behind a tree trunk or a car, waiting until she was distracted before they pounced.

Her hands were shoved deep into her pockets, and her fingers curled around the small box as though it possessed the ability to protect her from all the evil in the world. It was silly of course, it hadn't done anything to save her from anything that had happened to her so far, and yet whenever she was scared she couldn't help but reach for it.

Spooked and cold, she picked up the pace as she turned around and continued walking toward the light. It was like a lighthouse, a beacon, calling out to her, and when she got closer she saw that it was a diner. Did she have enough money for something to eat? She was starving, she hadn't eaten in two days, and all she'd had to drink was water from the tap in the bathroom when the bus stopped at a gas station. She was dying for a steaming hot cup of tea. She'd take that over something to eat because her stomach seemed to have become accustomed to the gnawing hunger and it no longer bothered her too much, being able to curl her cold hands around a hot mug, that offered her comfort that food couldn't right now.

Pulling out the last of her money, she had three dollar bills and a handful of change, probably not enough for a meal, but she should be able to get her cup of tea. Feeling better, she pushed open the door and stepped inside. It was warm in the diner, and immediately she felt herself relax a little. This town was small, no one would find her here, she could take some time, regroup, try to figure out a plan, and for now she could just sit indoors, out of the cold, and drink her tea.

The place was full, but she saw a booth in the back corner that was perfect for her, so she hurried over to it, sliding down onto a bench that was so much more comfortable than the cramped bus seat she had been stuck in for days.

It was warm enough in here that she could take off her coat, and she was just sliding her arms out when a pretty young waitress came bustling over.

"Evening." The woman smiled at her. "What can I get for you?"

"Evening," Meadow murmured back. It felt odd speaking to someone else because she hadn't spoken a word to anyone since she bought her ticket at the station over forty-eight hours ago. "How much is a cup of tea?" she asked anxiously, hoping she had enough. It would be embarrassing to have to say she couldn't afford it, and have to walk out of this nice warm place and back out into the cold night.

"Three dollars," the woman replied. Then her forehead creased with concern. "Is that all you want? Kitchen is still open, we have the best pumpkin soup you'll even find in your life. It's only five dollars for a nice big bowl and a slice of my Grandma's homemade bread. Or we have some delicious toasted sandwiches.

I could do you a grilled cheese or something?"

The woman looked at her expectantly, and Meadow felt her cheeks heat in embarrassment. It was obvious to the waitress that she was hungry and no doubt she looked dirty too, since it had been days since she showered, and the food she had mentioned sounded delicious, but she only had enough for the tea. "Just the tea please," she replied, hoping the woman didn't push further.

"Okay then." The waitress pasted on a smile that looked fake and breezed off.

Meadow had to fight back another batch of tears that threatened to burst out. It was humiliating enough to know that people could tell she was some poor homeless woman, but she wasn't going to add to that by crying in a diner full of people. So she sucked in her bottom lip and chewed on it, and tried to focus on the positives in her life instead of the negatives.

Not that there were many.

That reality brought fresh tears to her eyes, and she might have succumbed to them if the waitress hadn't reappeared. "Here you go, a nice hot cup of tea. We do free refills, and we're open until ten, so you can stay here as long as you like."

The woman's words were kind and compassionate, and Meadow knew that she was trying to be helpful, but all they did was fill her with shame.

She had no skills, no real education, no place to go to sleep tonight, and no money to buy food. How long did she really expect to last out here on her own?

"Th-thank you," she mumbled and fixed her gaze on the steam, which was twirling in little dancing puffs as it poured off the cup.

"You're welcome," the waitress replied before buzzing off to another table.

This was her life now, for at least as long as it took to find a way to fix things, so she may as well learn to make the best of it. She curled her hands around the mug, enjoying the way it burned a little, for now at least she could just enjoy the warmth of the diner and her cup of tea.

* * * * *

7:34 P.M.

He had noticed her the second she walked through the door.

It wasn't like she was hard to miss. Long blonde hair pulled back into a ponytail, blue eyes that darted nervously about as though she expected a monster to come jumping out at any second. Paper pale skin that hinted that she spent little time outdoors, dressed in jeans, a pink sweater, and cream-colored coat that looked as though they'd been slept in. Add the fear that was written all over the girl's face, and the fact that she appeared to be at least five months pregnant, and it didn't take a genius to figure out that she was in trouble.

Sheriff Abe Black stretched in his seat at the counter and tried as surreptitiously as he could to get another look at her. She had slipped onto the bench of the booth in the corner of the room furthest from the door, and scrunched herself right up into the corner, as though if it was possible she would make herself disappear altogether.

The girl looked young, nothing more than a kid. Was she a minor? Kicked out by her parents because she was pregnant? Abused by a parent or family member or friend, and wound up pregnant because of the abuse? Raped? A runaway who had been forced into prostitution only to wind up pregnant by a client?

His cop mind couldn't help but run through a million possibilities as he watched her.

She was just taking off her coat when Penny approached her. Abe watched their exchange, trying to gauge whether his gut reaction that the kid was in trouble and needed help was correct. It was busy in here tonight, and he couldn't hear what either

Penny or the girl were saying over the lively chatter, but the girl's cheeks suddenly went red, and he wondered if she was broke. Broke and pregnant wasn't a good combination for anyone let alone some kid.

"Penny," he called out as the waitress headed back toward the kitchen.

"What's up, Sheriff?" she asked as she came over. "Need a refill on that coffee? Another muffin? More soup?"

"No, I'm fine," he assured her. He liked Penny, in a purely platonic way, they had grown up together, gone to school together, even exchanged a kiss at an eighth grade make-out party, and he knew the mom of four little ones—two sets of twins under four—would tell him exactly what she thought of the pregnant kid. "The girl over there," he nodded his head in the direction of the girl's booth, "what did she say to you?"

"Not a lot," Penny said, giving him a refill of coffee he didn't need. He'd already consumed enough caffeine today to keep him up for the next three days straight. "She asked for a cup of tea, she looked hungry, and she's pregnant so I offered her something to eat, she said no, she just wanted the tea."

"Why do you think that is?"

Penny's brown eyes went sharp as she realized she was being interrogated. "Same reason you do I'd reckon."

"You think she's homeless?"

"I think there's only one reason a pregnant woman would turn down a bowl of hot soup and some homemade bread on a cold winter's night, and that's because she can't afford it."

"How old do you think she is?" Abe asked. He couldn't disagree with what Penny had just said. If the girl didn't like pumpkin soup she could have said so and asked for something else, but she'd turned down everything, the kid was definitely broke.

"Twenty maybe," Penny replied.

"Not younger?" He'd been hoping that if she was a kid he

7

could call in child protective services, have them drive out here in the morning and pick her up, maybe ask his parents if she could spend the night with them. But if the girl was an adult then he couldn't very well just walk up to her and demand that she tell him why she was pregnant and starving with no money to buy food.

"I don't think so, but those eyes." Penny paused and looked thoughtful. "They look haunted, and she seems scared. I'd say she needs help."

While he didn't disagree with her, he was the local sheriff, not the local busybody, and his job didn't give him the right to go up to strangers who hadn't done anything wrong and interrogate them, even if it *was* in their best interest. "Take her a bowl of soup, a grilled cheese sandwich, and a white chocolate and raspberry muffin. Tell her that it's nearly closing time and that you have to throw away any food that's left over at the end of the day so she's doing you a favor by taking it." Abe reached into his back pocket and pulled out some cash, handing it over to Penny. He might not be able to interrogate the woman, but he certainly wasn't the kind of man who would let a starving pregnant woman in need of help go off into the night with an empty stomach.

"You're a sweetheart, you know that." Penny leaned over and kissed his cheek, then took the money. "Beneath that tough exterior you put on there's a big, cuddly teddy bear lurking inside."

Abe certainly wouldn't go that far, but his parents had raised him right. They'd taught him to think of others before himself, and to always help someone in need if he was in a position to do so. He'd served in the military before becoming a cop, saving and protecting people was a part of him, it was written into his DNA, but he didn't think anyone would describe him as either a sweetheart or a big, cuddly teddy bear. He was too gruff, too brisk, too hard, and while he was able to soften himself when dealing with victims of crime, he didn't have a tender bone in his body.

"Don't even bother denying it." Penny grinned when he opened his mouth to protest. "You forget I've known you all your life. You're a good guy, Abe, a good guy with a big heart, and there's nothing wrong with letting everybody know it."

"Well don't let the girl know it," he reminded her. He wasn't after the kid's gratitude, he just wanted to do what he could to help her out, and if buying her a meal and letting her think that the food would go to waste if she didn't eat it helped her then he was all for it. That did *not* make him a big, cuddly teddy bear.

"I won't," Penny said with a laugh as she headed off to prepare the girl's food.

He didn't feel good about just giving her a meal and then sending her off into the night. What if she was in trouble? What if she was in danger? If she was running from an abusive ex or family member, then there was a chance they might come after her, especially since the baby could be proof of the abuse.

Or she was just a girl who got pregnant and embarrassed for anyone else to find out so she had decided to run away. It was sad, and she obviously needed help, but he was a cop not a social worker, and he had no proof that any sort of crime had occurred.

Let it go, he told himself. He'd done all he could for her. She had made her choices, and she had to live with the consequences, and if she was a victim of a crime there was nothing stopping her from going to the cops and getting the help she needed.

Abe watched as Penny carried a tray full of a huge bowl of soup—a bowl he knew was twice the usual size—homemade bread, sandwiches, and at least three muffins. He couldn't help but smile, Penny called him a sweetheart, but she and her family were some of the sweetest people he had ever met. They clearly wanted to do their own part in making sure the woman got the meal she obviously needed.

When Penny set the tray down the girl immediately shook her head and held out her hand, trying to stop Penny from unloading it. Penny said something, and he could see on the girl's face that she was having an internal battle, no doubt about accepting the food which she probably suspected wasn't really going to be thrown away, but eventually with a shy smile, she nodded.

Penny left her with the food and the girl immediately started eating, her hand was shaking so much he saw soup slosh over the side of her spoon, and he wondered how long it had been since she'd had a meal.

He couldn't help but smile as he watched her eat, glad that he'd been able to do something to help someone in need.

A good deed a day kept the anger away.

And he really did have a lot of anger inside, more than he could ever erase no matter how many good deeds he committed.

* * * * *

9:57 P.M.

Her time was up.

It was nearly ten, which meant that it was time to leave the diner's warmth and security and head out into the cold night. She still had no idea where she was going to go or how she was going to survive a night out on the street. She'd never done that before, she'd spent her first night in the bus station, then the last few nights she'd had the safety of the bus to protect her from the elements, but tonight she had no place to go.

Which meant she would be sleeping on the streets.

Meadow was terrified by the prospect.

First off there was the obvious problem of the cold, it was winter, and all she had to keep herself and her unborn baby warm was a coat that wasn't designed to take the place of a house and a bed. And second, she would have no protection from anyone who might be out wandering the streets at night.

What if there was a rapist out there?

She would be of no use to a thief, but maybe that would make the person angry, and they'd beat her up because she didn't have any money to give them.

With a last longing look at the diner—which was mostly empty now—Meadow shrugged back into her coat and stepped outside. At least she had been able to eat a good meal, and she wasn't hungry any longer. She wasn't really sure that she believed the whole whatever food that wasn't sold by the end of the day was thrown away story that Penny the waitress had told her, but in the end she had been too hungry to put up much resistance. Now she had a tummy full of soup and delicious homemade bread, and a muffin for dessert, plus she still had two sandwiches and two muffins left over which were packed in a paper bag that she was clutching tightly in her hand. When you had basically nothing what little you did have suddenly became very precious, and right now those couple of sandwiches and muffins were all she had to eat for the foreseeable future.

As well as getting something to eat, she'd also been able to use the bathroom at the diner, and it was so nice to use a clean restroom after the ones from the gas stations these last few days. This one had been painted a warm, cheery yellow, the floor was the same hardwood as the rest of the diner, the toilet had been clean, and there was a vase of flowers sitting on the vanity, and a soft white towel to dry her hands with. It was heaven.

But that was over now.

She could hardly sit in the diner all day every day, and she couldn't expect that they would give her free food every day, so she was going to have to make her sandwiches and muffins last as long as she could. She didn't even have enough left for another cup of tea, so there wasn't even that to look forward to.

Maybe in the morning she would walk up and down the street, see what stores River's End had, and if any of them were in the market for a new employee. She had no experience, but she was hardworking and she paid great attention to detail, she was a quick learner, and she was willing to do anything she was asked to. If she could just earn enough to buy even one meal a day she'd be happy, and maybe she could save up a little, find a room to rent, or buy a bus ticket and move on. She didn't really care which.

The street was quiet, but the occasional car drove past, and there was a couple walking hand in hand further down the street. She stared wistfully at them, all she had ever wanted, for as long as she could remember, was someone to love her. She just wanted a place in the world where she belonged, but no matter how hard she searched for it she could never find it.

Still, that was a worry for another day. Right now, keeping herself and her unborn baby alive was the most important thing, it hardly mattered about finding someone who would love her forever if she was dead.

Hunching over against the wind that had blown up while she was in the diner, Meadow started walking down the street. She had no idea what she was looking for, maybe a church with an open door, or an alley that would block some of the wind, or even a large bush or something that she could curl up underneath.

She was about halfway down the street when she saw an alley. This would be a nice quiet place to spend the night. It was narrow, barely wide enough for a car, and there was a dumpster down toward the end, it would be smelly, but she could move it forward a little and then get in between the dumpster and the wall, and that should provide shelter from the wind and enough warmth that she didn't freeze to death out here.

That was a possibility.

Even if she could find a job tomorrow she wasn't going to be paid right away. It could be days or most likely weeks before she had enough to be able to rent a room, and just because there hadn't been any snow in a week didn't mean it wasn't coming. There was a good chance that someone would find her body one morning after she had succumbed to hypothermia overnight.

But not tonight.

She had no intention of dying tonight.

Or any night.

She had a little baby that was relying on her to keep it alive, at least until it was born, after that she didn't know what she was going to do with it. Part of her wanted to keep it, but the sensible part of her brain knew that she couldn't even take care of herself right now. How was she going to raise a baby? She couldn't keep it out here on the streets, and what if she decided to move on again? She could hardly drag an infant from town to town while she tried to find a place where she felt safe enough to settle down.

Again she pushed that worry away. She was only five months pregnant so she had another four months to go before she had to worry about whether or not she was going to keep her baby or drop it off at a hospital, police station, or fire station. She knew about the safe haven laws that allowed a parent to drop off an unharmed infant without fear of being charged with a crime.

Today though, her biggest worry was making it till morning.

The further she walked down the alley the more the wind died down. That was definitely a good sign. Luck was on her side again when she reached the dumpster, it was large and she wasn't sure she would be able to move it on her own, but it must have been emptied within the last twenty-four hours or so because it was mostly empty and rolled easily away from the wall.

Needing its protection, Meadow didn't move it too far away from the wall, just enough for her to wriggle in between. The ground was cold and dirty, and she didn't want to lie down, so instead she shuffled about so that she was resting against the wall. It wasn't comfortable, but at least she thought she would be warm enough down here.

She yawned. A big one that stretched her mouth as far open as it would go, she was so tired, she hadn't slept much on the bus, she kept expecting someone to come storming after her, having somehow managed to track her down. Just because he hadn't so far didn't mean that he wouldn't. He was smart, much smarter than she had realized, and she wouldn't put it past him to figure out a way to find her.

As soon as she closed her eyes her mind filled with fears.

All the things she had run away from, all the uncertainties that her future held, all the fears that something would go wrong with her pregnancy and her baby would die, all the things that could happen to her living out on the streets.

So many fears.

For about the tenth time today tears brimmed in her eyes. She couldn't do this; she wasn't strong enough to do this. How had she ever thought that this was going to work out?

It wasn't.

It couldn't.

She wasn't strong enough to do this.

She wasn't smart enough to do this.

This was a mistake.

Only there was no way to take it back. She couldn't go backward, and yet she didn't know how to go forward.

Where did that leave her?

One hand lifted to touch the brick wall she was resting against, the other touched the back of the dumpster. She was stuck between a rock and a hard place, that was where it left her.

* * * * *

10:38 P.M.

He loved small-town life.

Abe sat on his front porch, looking out at the quiet night. It was dark out, the sky was filled with thick clouds, obscuring any light the moon might have given, but he had the light on in the living room behind him, and he was enjoying just rocking slowly back and forth on the porch swing and watching as the wind rustled through the forest.

He couldn't imagine living anywhere else.

Small town life was quiet and simple. River's End was busy in the winter as families flocked to come skiing, in the summer people came to go camping, hiking, and swimming and do water sports on the lake, but the rest of the year it was peaceful here.

Just the way he liked it.

His dad had been in the military, but after being discharged the family had moved here when he was eight, and this was where he had grown up. Running through the forest, climbing trees, snowball fights in the winter, long summer days playing in the river, bonfires in the fall, it had been perfect. His family had its issues like any other, but he'd had a happy childhood, and after he had done a tour in Afghanistan, he hadn't been able to think of any place he'd rather start his own life than right back here. So he'd become a cop, bought this plot of land just a couple of miles north of town, and now he was the sheriff, and it was his job to make sure that this place remained a paradise for all the generations of kids to come.

Thinking of kids made him think of the girl from the diner, not that his thoughts had strayed far from her since he'd seen her come walking in. She was a beautiful young woman, and he hoped that whatever had led to her being pregnant and homeless would work itself out. Hopefully, friends or family would track her down and take her home, support her through whatever had led her to run away, and that everything would work out for her and her baby.

But lingering at the back of his mind was that there was a more sinister reason for her being homeless. There were so many people out there who would take advantage of a pretty girl, and he hoped that wasn't what had happened to her.

Meadow.

Her name was Meadow.

Penny had managed to pry out of the girl her name when she'd given her the tray full of food. It was a beautiful name for a beautiful girl, and the image of the smile on her face when she had accepted the dinner and started eating it was wedged firmly into his mind, and he couldn't seem to dislodge it no matter how hard he tried.

Abe might have sat on the porch, another cup of coffee in his hand, the wind whistling through the trees, for hours, but his phone buzzed, and as the sheriff he never ignored a call, so he pulled it out of his pocket.

"Sheriff Black," he said into it.

"Hey, Abe, sorry to bother you so late, but we had a call from Mrs. DuVall. She said she was working late and she heard someone moving about in the alley behind her store," his deputy sheriff, also his cousin, Julian, told him.

"Is she sure?" It wasn't that he thought Mrs. DuVall was lying, but the woman did have a tendency to be a bit of a drama queen, and he wouldn't have been surprised if she had blown the whole thing out of proportion.

"Sounded pretty certain. The Tyler kids have been running wild through the town late at night, and she thought it might have been them up to mischief."

By running wild what Mrs. DuVall really meant was that the Tyler kids were going through a rough time, their mom was dying of cancer, and their dad was away a lot because he traveled for work, so they had been acting out and riding their snowmobiles up and down Main Street late at night. The way Mrs. DuVall said it you'd think they were breaking into stores and trashing them or beating people up. "You'd think she could be a little more understanding given their situation," he said.

"You'd think," Julian agreed. "You want me to go check it out?"

"No, I'll go," he replied, already standing and heading back inside to grab a coat and his keys.

"All right, call if it's anything."

"Sure," he said, but he was positive it wasn't going to turn out to be anything. "See you tomorrow."

Besides his cousin, there were two other deputies in River's End, Julian's brother Will, and his youngest brother's best friend, Fletcher Harris. There was also a pretty young woman, Poppy Deveraux, who answered the phones and managed the office. Although that was enough for the quieter months, in the busier months he sometimes wished they had another deputy or two, and he was hoping to hire someone else in the summer.

Inside, he put out the fire that was crackling away in his living room fireplace, then left a light on so it wouldn't be pitch black by the time he returned. His cabin was about two and a half miles from the town, maybe a five-minute drive, so he didn't bother grabbing gloves and a scarf, he should be fine with just his coat.

The cold usually didn't bother him much, and since the drive was short, he didn't bother turning on the heat. By the time his SUV warmed up enough for the heater to do any good he'd basically be there anyway.

By the time he reached Main Street and parked his car the wind had picked up some more, and it blew straight through him almost making him regret his decision not to put on a beanie or scarf or something. There were no kids riding snowmobiles up and down the street, in fact there was no one. Anywhere. The place was completely quiet. The diner was closed, and the other restaurant in town was over in the hotel a mile outside the town on the south end, so there were no people about, walking to their cars, or lingering in the street kissing or making out.

Abe nearly decided to just get back in his car and head home. He had a little work to attend to before he went to bed, and he usually liked to work late then go for a long run before he even attempted to try to sleep. He'd seen a lot in his tour of Afghanistan, and while it didn't usually bother him during the day, those unresolved feelings sometimes came out at night in the form of nightmares. The nightmare was always the same, the bassinette with the baby in it, only it was his baby, and no matter how many times he tried to get it out before the bomb went off he always failed.

He'd do a quick check of the alley where Mrs. DuVall claimed she had heard someone and then he'd go home, text Julian that he could assure the older woman who ran the art gallery that there was no one out there. The alley was quiet, he didn't see anyone, he didn't hear anything, and he was convinced it was the wind that had created the noise Mrs. DuVall had heard, but then he saw something.

Someone had moved the dumpster.

He noticed this because they'd been working a case where someone had been mugging tourists and dumping the empty wallets and purses in the dumpsters around the town. As a result he had spent a lot of time around the dumpsters, and this one had definitely been moved, it was usually situated right up against the back wall.

Abe walked closer, wondering whether the noise Mrs. DuVall had heard was another mugging and one that had progressed to the point of violence. He was sure it was only a matter of time before their thief progressed to assault and he half expected to see someone lying back here, beaten and unconscious.

But he didn't.

Instead, he saw the woman from the diner. She wasn't beaten up, and she didn't appear to be unconscious, but she did look like she was sleeping.

Guilt immediately began to poke at him.

He should have done more, he had suspected that the woman was homeless and had no place to go, but he hadn't wanted to interfere because she was an adult and there was no crime in not having a place to live. Now a pregnant woman was sleeping behind a dumpster in the middle of winter.

No good deed went unpunished.

Abe knew that and yet he also knew what he had to do. There was no way he was allowing this woman to continue to sleep outside, so even though he knew this probably wasn't going to turn out to be one of his best ideas, he didn't see any other option. And maybe if there was something sinister going on here—and his gut was telling him that there was—then he could find out what it was, find a way to help this girl so she could move on with her life.

With a sigh, he moved the dumpster further away and then crouched down beside Meadow and reached out, gently grasping her shoulder and giving a small shake.

"Meadow, wake up," he said, keeping his voice quiet so as not to frighten her. "Meadow, I'm the sheriff, wake up now. Meadow."

* * * * *

10:56 P.M.

Someone was touching her.

Meadow woke in a panic.

He was here.

She was in trouble.

She shouldn't have run.

What was he going to do to her?

Although she knew it was a bad idea, and one that was going to serve no purpose but to heap punishment on top of punishment, she couldn't go back without a fight.

So a fight is what she put up.

She screamed, she thrashed, she swung her arms and kicked her feet, but it didn't seem to do any good. Instead of doing anything to stop him, she was dragged out from where she had burrowed herself away and pinned against a chest that felt every bit as hard as the wall she had just been lying against. Strong arms encircled her, pinning her own arms to her sides and holding her in place.

She gave up.

What was the point in fighting?

She had done the wrong thing in running away, and she was going to be punished for it. Why continue to make it worse?

"It's okay," a voice was murmuring in her ear. "You're okay, I'm not going to hurt you. I'm the sheriff. My name is Abe, Abe Black. You're okay, Meadow."

He knew her name.

How did he know her name?

She didn't know him so how could he possibly know her?

Was he here to take her back?

She would rather live on the street, sleeping behind dumpsters, even after her baby was born than she would go back to that place.

She started to fight again, she wouldn't go back, she wouldn't, she *wouldn't*.

"Shh, stopping fighting me, I don't want to hurt you. Are you hearing me? Whoever you think I am, I'm not. I'm the sheriff here."

Sheriff?

He was a cop?

Cops were good, right?

So if this man wasn't lying and really was a cop, then he didn't mean her any harm.

Slowly she stopped fighting, letting herself go limp as she rested back against the strong chest. She was breathing heavily, and her heart hammered in her chest like a jackhammer. It took a moment for her to get herself under control, but the man didn't seem to mind, he loosened his grip on her, but his arms still circled around her.

"Your name is Meadow, right?" he asked. When she nodded he continued, "I was in the diner earlier when you were in there. I saw you talking with Penny when she gave you your meal. I hadn't seen you around River's End before so I asked her your name."

That made sense.

It was a perfectly reasonable and logical way that he could have found out her name, and yet history had taught her to always expect something bad so this was no exception.

She was about to make him show her his badge or whatever it was that would prove he wasn't lying and really was the sheriff when she realized something. He had been in the diner when she had been there, and she thought she vaguely recalled seeing a big man with red hair and a red beard sitting at the counter, and he had been watching when Penny brought her the food. She'd been suspicious then, but now she realized that the food wasn't brought to her to prevent waste, this man had paid for it and asked Penny to deliver it to her.

"The soup, and the sandwiches, you sent them to me," she said softly.

"You looked hungry," he said, confirming her suspicions.

That was sweet of him.

Really sweet.

She was a stranger, he shouldn't have noticed her at all let alone managed to figure out that she was hungry and do something about it.

"Thank you," she said. It didn't seem like enough but what else could she do? She didn't have anything to give him but her gratitude and that he could have in spades. "That was so nice of you."

"You're welcome," he said, finally releasing her and standing, offering her his hand.

Meadow hesitated but decided she had nothing to lose and this man seemed to be trustworthy, so she took his hand and allowed him to pull her to her feet. It was the fact that he had not only bought food for her but been thoughtful enough to try to make sure she wasn't embarrassed by telling the waitress to tell her the food was going in the bin if it wasn't eaten. To pay attention to something so small as her feelings he'd have to be a good guy.

Right?

Nervous and embarrassed for him to know what a mess she had made of her life, that she was pregnant and homeless, with no place to go and no money to buy food, she fixed her gaze on the dirty ground and waited to see what he was going to do.

"Would you like to come and spend the night at my place? I have a spare room, and you can't stay out here, it's winter, and you're pregnant, so you're welcome to come home with me, take a shower, have a hot meal if you're still hungry, spend the night in the spare room, then we can talk in the morning, figure out a more long term plan."

She just stared at him.

Had he just asked her to go home with him?

She couldn't go home with him, she didn't even know him. He was a stranger, and it was trusting a stranger who seemed trustworthy that had gotten her into this mess in the first place.

And yet what else could she do?

She couldn't stay out here, and the idea of a shower was a tempting one. To scrub every inch of her skin and wash her hair, it sounded delightful, and it was enough to have her wavering. Maybe she could go, have a shower and a meal, sleep in a real bed, and then she could be gone in the morning before the sun rose.

"I don't have anything to pay you with," she said, then lifted her hand where there was a diamond ring on one of her fingers, it wasn't much, but she had been wearing it when she ran, and it was at least something. "I could give you this," she said, pulling it off and holding it out so he could see it. "It's not much, the diamond is small, but it's all I have to pay you with."

The man—Abe she thought he'd said his name was—took the ring and Meadow was sure he was going to accept it as payment for his generous offer. But instead of pocketing it, he reached out and took hold of her hand, sliding the ring back onto her finger.

"I'm not doing this because I want you to pay me back. You need help, I'm in a position to be able to offer you the help that you need. You don't have to give me anything in return."

"But," she began in protest. In her experience no one was that generous. If she took him up on the offer she suspected he would end up wanting something in return. If it wasn't cash or jewelry, then she suspected she knew what it was.

"No buts, you can't stay out here all night, so if you're willing, let's head back to my place," he said gruffly.

Despite the gruff tone he had done two nice things for her now, he'd bought her dinner and tried to make sure she wouldn't feel embarrassed about a stranger paying for her food, and now he was offering up his home to her so she wouldn't have to sleep on the street. It was clear he felt sorry for her, but was pride enough to keep her from accepting this generous offer?

Although she knew that she was putting herself in a potentially vulnerable position, she would be alone and at the mercy of a man who was so much bigger than she was, he had been nice to her, and she thought that she could trust him. He was a sheriff after all.

"Okay," she agreed, still a little hesitant. "Th-thank you, that's really nice of you."

"Just doing my job," he said briskly, shrugging out of his coat and draping it over her shoulders. "Let's get going, you're cold, we should get you indoors as quickly as possible."

With that, he turned and started walking down the alley. Meadow trailed along behind him, still wondering if this was a good idea but making no move to say no or tell him that she couldn't go with him.

She didn't have good instincts.

She had made mistakes in her life.

She had regrets.

Some which would follow her around for the rest of her life, and going home with this man, who she knew absolutely nothing about, might end up being the biggest regret of her life.

But it didn't feel wrong.

It felt right.

A shower, a meal, a bed, the simple things in life, but the ones she had been missing the most. Then after she had a good night's sleep she could be gone and out of here before he was even out of bed.

Or maybe she would finally find the one thing she had been searching for her whole life.

Love.

That was all she wanted—it was all *anyone* wanted—to be loved and to love in return.

Maybe this tough, gruff, but sweet guy would be the one to love her.

Or she would have tempted fate too many times, and he would be the one to finally destroy her.

* * * * *

11:19 P.M.

Why was he doing this again?

What made him think this was a good idea?

Abe knew that when his two younger brothers found out that he had brought a woman home to stay with him, he was never going to hear the end of it.

If his parents found out, his mother would be planning a wedding before he could blink no matter how many times he told her that he was just helping out a person in need. He was thirty-three and the oldest of four kids, none of whom were married, and his mom wanted grandbabies while she was still young enough to enjoy them.

Although he didn't want to burst his mom's bubble, he didn't foresee a wife and kids in his future. He'd been married once, and he'd been burned. It wasn't an experience that he wished to repeat, not even to give the mother he adored the grandchildren she longed for.

Meadow was quiet in the car's passenger seat, and Abe cast a surreptitious glance her way. She was sitting straight, her back pressed up against the leather seat, her ankles were crossed, and her hands were folded and resting in her lap. She was nervous, anxious, and yet she had trusted him. She didn't know him and yet she had willingly got into the car with him and accepted his offer, so despite what had happened to her, she hadn't lost her faith in mankind.

He liked that.

He respected that.

He wished he could have that same attitude.

"So," he said slowly, hoping to break the tension and put Meadow at ease, and to find out a little bit more about her, "I know your name is Meadow, but that's all I know about you."

She began to fidget, picking at the hem of her coat. "My last name is Smith, I'm twenty-four and pregnant," she said, stating the obvious as she rested her shaking hands on her stomach. "I don't know, that's it I guess."

So much for trying to find out more about her, still having her in his house would certainly help him get her talking.

He hoped.

Because Meadow couldn't live with him forever.

He needed to find out who was responsible for hurting her because she was a victim—he was as sure of that as he was that she was sitting beside him—and he had to save victims.

Save them and send them on their way.

"Here we are," he said as he turned off the tree-lined road and up into his driveway.

When he parked in front of his cabin Meadow clapped her hands in delight. "Oh, it's so cute."

"It's a nice cabin," he agreed. When he had moved back here after leaving the military, he and his dad and brothers had built this place themselves. Every time he came here he felt that connection to his family. Family was important, family was there for you when you had to pick up the pieces of a shattered life, family was what rallied around you and helped you rebuild that shattered life.

"Do you live here alone?" Meadow asked, but there was no fear in her face or her voice, he didn't know why she wasn't afraid of him, but he took that as a sign that she was going to be okay.

"Yes, just me," he said as he turned off the engine and got out, walking around to open her door for her, his mother had taught him to be chivalrous. Meadow climbed out of the car as soon as he opened the door, but she didn't move toward the house. It was like she was awaiting permission and his suspicions that she had been abused grew. "I'll give you the grand tour."

When he started walking she followed suit, trailing along behind him up the steps and across the porch. Since this was River's End he hadn't bothered locking the house, so he opened the front door right up and stepped into the hall. Meadow followed and stood silently beside him, waiting for him to take the lead.

"Stairs lead up to the second floor. My bedroom is the one on the right so you can take the spare bedroom on the left. It has its own bathroom so you can have some privacy while you take a bath or a shower, I'll get you clean towels from the linen closet, and I think there are some of my mom's toiletries from when she and my dad stayed here while they had their place repainted up there, I'm sure she won't mind you using them. Down here the living room is on the right, you can watch some TV or use the laptop if you want, and the kitchen is on the left, there's a laundry room off it, and we can throw your things in the washer, I'll give you some sweats to wear. If you're hungry I can make you something to eat, or you're welcome to make yourself something."

"I am a little hungry," she said. Her blue eyes watched the floor intently, then popped up briefly to meet his like she might be told that she shouldn't be hungry after eating earlier.

"Why don't you go and look in the cupboards, see what you want, and I'll pop upstairs and grab something for you to change into after you take a shower." He wasn't usually the one who dealt with victims in cases. It wasn't that he was bad at it, it was just that he was much more comfortable with people who didn't need handholding than those who did. And he suspected that despite her trusting nature, Meadow Smith needed quite a lot of handholding.

"Are you sure it's okay for me to go looking through your kitchen?" Meadow asked timidly.

"Sunshine, if it wasn't okay I wouldn't have said it." He winked at her, then headed up the stairs. His mom was good with people, and she was in need of a new project now that the youngest Black child, Dahlia, had moved away permanently. He knew that Mom had been hoping to convince Dahlia to come back here after she graduated but that was never going to happen. Maybe tomorrow he'd speak with his mother, see if she wouldn't mind spending a little time with Meadow, maybe with another woman she'd be more likely to open up.

Abe opened his closet door and grabbed an old sweatshirt and a pair of sweatpants. They'd be several sizes too big and she'd practically be swimming in them, but they would do for now. When he spoke with his mom in the morning he'd ask her if Dahlia had left any clothes behind that Meadow could borrow, she was about the same size as his sister, and they'd do until he got a chance to take her shopping.

Take her shopping.

He was acting like there was something between them that went beyond just him helping her out. That had to stop because there wasn't anything more to it. Meadow was a beautiful woman, and now that he knew she was older than he'd first thought, he couldn't deny that he was attracted to her, but he wasn't looking for anything beyond a roll in the hay, and she was in no position for that kind of thing.

Taking the clothes with him, he headed back downstairs where he found Meadow standing at the counter chopping vegetables. She didn't notice him right away, and he took a moment to just stand and watch her. Her face had relaxed, and she chopped with practiced ease that suggested she did this often.

She straightened and turned to pick up the pot she'd put next to the stove when she saw him. "Uh, I found some vegetables in your fridge, I hope it's okay to use them."

Abe strolled over and took a seat at the table. "What did I say, sunshine?"

"That I could go and look in the cupboards, see what I want," she said, and it didn't go unnoticed that she quoted him word for word.

"There you go then. Here are the clothes, sorry they'll be too big for you, but they'll do for tonight. When you take a shower leave the dirty clothes outside the bathroom door, and I'll throw them in the washer. What are you making?"

"I'm going to cook the vegetables in a little water, just until they start to soften, then I'll add a little flour, just enough to thicken it a bit, then I'm going to put them on some pastry in a pie pan, make a kind of vegetable pie," she explained, her azure eyes twinkling.

"You like cooking," he said, it was written all over her face, and that gave him an idea. She had been uncomfortable about not being able to pay him something, he was sure that she would love it if he could get her a job, and he knew just the place.

Meadow paused, an odd look crossing her face and she nodded slowly. "I guess I do," she said like she had never even thought about it before. "I'm making enough for two, if you want some," she said, giving him a shy smile.

"Sounds nice," he said, smiling back and hoping that his decision to help her didn't end up hurting her instead. She was looking at him like he was her Prince Charming, riding in on a white horse to make all her problems go away and that couldn't be further from the truth.

He wasn't a prince.

He was a gruff, emotionally distant bachelor who enjoyed his privacy.

FEBRUARY 4TH

2:37 A.M.

The whip whistled as it flew through the air.

Even though she had been expecting it, the sting as it made contact with her bare skin made her wince and cry out.

She knew it was a bad idea, she knew it was only going to make him angry, she knew it was only going to lead to more pain, but there was only so much she could take, and Carla had already well and truly reached her limit.

His hand curled around her neck, and he squeezed enough to make it difficult for her to draw a full breath. She would have clawed at his hand, tried to get it away from her neck but she couldn't. He had tied her wrists together with rope that dug into her flesh every time she moved, then secured them above her head so they were stretched tight. He had barely given her enough space to stand flat on her feet and every time he hit her and she stumbled, it yanked painfully on her shoulders.

"Did I give you permission to make a sound?" he growled at her, his face so close to hers that she could feel his breath hot and putrid on her skin, and he spat a little as he spoke.

How did she answer that?

If she assumed that was permission to speak and answered, but he hadn't really wanted her to then she would be punished again.

But if she assumed he wanted her to remain silent, and she didn't answer, but he really had wanted her to then she would be punished.

It was a no-win situation.

Her whole life was beginning to feel like one great, big no-win situation. Damned if she did and damned if she didn't.

Deciding she would wait to see if he was going to give her a clue as to what he wanted from her she just stood there, trembling, silent tears rolling down her cheeks, breathing heavily from pain and fear.

"I asked you a question," he roared, picking up a pair of pliers and putting them on one of her nipples and twisting so hard she shrieked. "Another sound? Did I ask you to make a sound?"

Carla shook her head as she wobbled, trying to get her footing as her body instinctively tried to move away from the pliers that were inflicting such horrific pain.

"You will learn," he said, dropping the pliers and letting them fall to the floor where they landed with a clunk. "I am in control here. You do not do anything, *anything*, without my permission. You are mine, you came to me willingly, now I get to do with you whatever I want."

She *had* come here willingly.

What a fool she had been.

If she had known what he was really like then she would never have come.

It had been a mistake, and one that she would no doubt regret for the rest of her life.

Her no doubt *short* life.

Abruptly, he released the rope attaching her wrists to the ceiling, and unbalanced, she dropped to her knees.

"That's right," he goaded her, "kneel before me. Kneel before your master. Kiss my feet," he ordered.

Too afraid to do anything but what he told her to, she leaned down, flinching at the pain in her back, which was covered in open, bloody welts that ripped further open at the movement, but managing to hold in any sounds that might have escaped, Carla touched her lips to his shoes. She had never been so humiliated in all her life, and knowing that she had brought all of this on herself made it all so much worse.

"There we go, that wasn't so hard, was it?" he asked.

It seemed like he wanted an answer when he asked her an outright question, so she said, "No."

"You'll learn," he told her, patting her head like she was a dog. "I'm going to train you just the way I want you, and soon you'll forget about the before. You'll forget who you were, you'll forget about your old life, you'll forget about everything but the fact that you are mine."

Just days ago she was a vibrant, happy college student. She was nineteen, she should have the whole world at her feet. She was an adult now, free to live on her own and make her own plans for her future. She had been excited about her classes, and she loved her job at the little boutique clothing store she worked at because the owner would give her discounts on the new season stock. She had everything, and now she had nothing.

Nothing but this man and his violent, sadistic whims.

This was her future.

"Get up," he ordered.

She did.

The path of least resistance was the one she was going to take.

She stood still while he bound her hands behind her back.

"Go over to the bed."

She did.

When she got to it she stopped and waited for her next instruction. She wasn't going to make a single move without him expressly telling her to.

"Lie down, on your stomach."

Doing so was difficult with her hands restrained behind, and she kind of flopped onto her stomach, making her back sting. She turned her head to the side so she could breathe and waited to see what kind of fresh hell awaited her next.

He stood beside the bed, and she could feel his eyes roaming her naked body. Even though she couldn't see him because her face was turned in the opposite direction, Carla knew his gaze lingered on the welts he had put on her skin. He liked that, he liked inflicting pain, liked knowing that she was hurting, and liked knowing that those marks would leave scars that would forever mar her flesh and soul.

Carla waited.

And waited.

And waited.

He knew that the longer he prolonged this, the more the anticipation of what horrid thing he was going to do would cause her anxiety. And it did. Her whole body was tense, she held herself stiffly like she could almost will herself to turn into a stone that he couldn't torment.

"You're a beautiful woman, Carla," he said, running his hand from her shoulder down her back, making sure that he ran his fingers over her open wounds so she winced in pain, then he let his hand come to rest on her bottom. "It's a shame you weren't a virgin though, I don't like that you lied about it."

She knew that.

She'd told him she was a virgin because she thought it was important to him, but when he found out that she wasn't he had lost it. He'd raped her so viciously he'd made her bleed and then when he was done, he had beaten her so badly that she was covered in bruises from head to toe, and even three days later had looked more like a black and blue tie-dye shirt than a person.

"But there's one hole left that can be mine," he said with a wicked laugh as his fingers moved to prod at that area.

Carla lost it.

He wasn't touching her there.

He wasn't.

He had taken enough from her, but she wasn't going to let him do that.

She flopped about looking like a dying fish as she struggled to get her battered and bruised body to cooperate so she could get off the bed. She was going to try to make a run for it, she wasn't just lying around and letting him use her as his own personal toy.

Somehow Carla managed to get off the bed, but she didn't make it far.

The whip rained down a bevy of blows on her back, her legs, her shoulders, she screeched and wept and begged, but the blows kept coming.

When he was done hitting her, he picked her up as though she was nothing more than a small child, reminding her once again how small she was in comparison to him. She was a little under five feet, but her height had never bothered her before, she hadn't minded the short jokes, and she had secretly enjoyed buying clothes in the kids' department sometimes because they were so cute and colorful. But now she wished she was big. Huge. Large enough to squash this wicked, evil man.

He tossed her down onto the bed and loomed above her. Obviously not wanting her to try running again, he untied the rope binding her wrists and then secured one end of it to the bedpost and the other around her left wrist. Then he shoved her into a kneeling position so her bare backside was on full display, ready and waiting for him to play his sick, twisted games.

Tears seeped from the corners of her eyes, which she had scrunched closed in the vain hope she could block him out. And then because he took pleasure in her pain, he didn't bother to use lubricant or move slowly, he just shoved himself inside her, splitting her body and her mind and soul into shreds.

* * * * *

5:50 A.M.

He hadn't slept a wink all night.

Abe had gone to bed after he and Meadow had eaten. Part of

him had anticipated that she would bolt as soon as she was clean and fed, but he'd heard her coming up the stairs and closing the bedroom door behind her, then the sound of the shower running. He had tossed and turned, listening to the water run through the pipes for almost an hour before he had come back downstairs and sat in the dark in the living room, wondering how this was all going to play out.

Sure he'd invited Meadow to stay with him, and he wasn't regretting it, it was the right thing to do, but he hadn't really thought it through. How long would she stay? Days? Weeks? Months? How was he going to get to the bottom of what led to her being on the street? He had no idea about Meadow's past so he didn't really know how she would react to him. Was she going to get overly attached to him? He didn't even know what her long term plan was.

She was still here, but for how long?

He knew she was embarrassed but whatever had led to her being out on the streets was nothing to be embarrassed about. The cop part of him wanted to keep questioning her, get to the bottom of things so he could fix them and then send her on her way. Maybe this morning he would try again to get a little information out of her while they ate breakfast, he wasn't the kind of guy who could just let things go, especially after the way she had reacted when he'd woken her up in the alley last night.

Okay, so being woken by a stranger while sleeping on the streets would be upsetting for anyone, but there was something about the fear on her face and the strength with which she had fought him that said she was afraid. She was running from someone, someone who terrified her, and the protective side of him wanted to find that person and punish them so Meadow could move on and feel safe.

Footsteps.

He could hear footsteps on the stairs.

Meadow was coming, but was she staying or making a run for

it?

She thought she was being quiet, but he had been in the military, he'd done a tour in a warzone, he noticed every little sound no matter how quiet.

Abe stood and walked to the living room door, watching in the shadows as Meadow tiptoed down the stairs. Obviously she intended to make a getaway while she thought he was still in bed.

Unluckily for her, he didn't give up on things that easily.

She was a case to him now, one that he wanted to solve, so until he had solved her problems she wasn't going anywhere.

"Morning, sunshine," he said.

Meadow was on the second last step and shrieked in surprise at his sudden presence. She lost her balance and stumbled, her arms wind-milling as she tried to regain it before she fell and landed on her backside.

He reached out and grabbed her shoulder, steadying her before she could fall. Her eyes lifted to meet his, and even though it was mostly dark in the house, he could tell that her cheeks had just gone bright red.

"Leaving me before the sun's up, sunshine?" he asked.

"I, uh, I was just, I didn't want to, I just thought, I'm sorry," she rambled, "I didn't mean to be rude, thank you so much for your hospitality. I'm sorry," she said again, and since his hand was still on her arm he felt her brace herself as though she expected that he would hit her for her perceived wrongdoing.

Abe sighed.

This wasn't what he wanted.

He wanted Meadow to be comfortable for as long as she was his guest here, and he wanted to help her. She was a sweet woman, and she was obviously in trouble, but he also found her attractive. She was older than he had first thought, not a kid, she'd told him she was twenty-four so she was only nine years younger than him, but Abe didn't think that given whatever had happened to her that she was interested in a fling.

And he only did flings.

Besides, she was pregnant, she no doubt wasn't interested in starting anything—however brief—with another man.

"Come and sit down," he said, guiding her down the last step and across the hall into the kitchen. "What do you like for breakfast?"

He had switched on the light as they entered the room and he saw that she looked almost confused by the question, like the idea that someone should be interested enough in her to ask what she wanted was perplexing to her. "Whatever you have is fine," she said in a small voice.

He was no psychologist, and he wasn't looking to be this woman's therapist as she worked through whatever issues she had, and yet at the same time he felt almost compelled to do whatever it took to help her. Keeping his voice firm but gentle, he repeated his question, "What do *you* like for breakfast."

"Well," she said hesitantly, "I like chocolate chip pancakes."

"Chocolate chip pancakes it is then." While he collected ingredients from the fridge and the cupboard, Meadow stood awkwardly in the middle of the room, right where he had left her when he'd released his hold on her arm. He was starting to see a pattern here. The fear, the lack of self-confidence, the loss of self, she had been abused, either by a boyfriend or husband, or by a parent or other male role model, or possibly both. "Meadow," he finally said when he couldn't take her staring anymore, "I told you last night, you're safe here. Whatever—whoever—you're running from you don't have to worry about here. I get that you've been hurt, but you decided to do something about it, you ran, now you can start rebuilding your life. You can stay here for as long as you like, and if you're interested, I spoke with someone in town, and I found you a job."

"A job?" she echoed, her eyes growing wide.

"As a cook. There's a huge hotel just south of town, and they have a restaurant. I'm friends with the owner, her name is Maggie, and I texted her after I brought you here last night. I thought that having a job might help you."

"You did that for me?" Those big wide eyes now grew watery with tears making them sparkly like the ocean.

He didn't want Meadow's gratitude, he just wanted to help her get on her feet, find who hurt her, and throw them in prison so she and her baby would be free. Brushing aside her thanks, he turned to the stove and began pouring out pancake batter. "She said that you should be there to help with the breakfast rush. I thought I'd drop you off on my way to work, around seven."

"Okay," she agreed.

"I don't need the money but if it will make you feel better once you get your first paycheck, you can pay rent or something."

"Yes," she said eagerly. "I want to do that. But are you sure you still … I mean last night you felt sorry for me because …" she looked down at her swollen belly. "If you've changed your mind I understand," she finished in a small voice.

Abe turned off the stove then walked over to Meadow. "Come and sit," he said, taking a seat at the table. "Look, Meadow, I offered to let you stay here, and I'm not going to change my mind on that. You can stay here for as long as you need until you get back on your feet. And I'm the sheriff, if you want to tell me what happened I can help you with that too. But don't make me out to be some sort of white knight hero, that's not who I am. Helping you is just the right thing to do." He didn't mean to sound so blunt, but he didn't want to give her the wrong impression. There was nothing heroic about this decision.

"Okay," she agreed again, nodding enthusiastically, but he could tell from the expression on her face that she hadn't really heard a word he'd said. She was looking at him with adoration, she saw him as her savior now, and he wasn't sure how to change that.

Send her off to live with someone else?

Kiss her like he wanted to every time he looked at her plump pink lips and then break her heart?

Tell her the truth about him so she would realize he was no hero?

Abe had no idea what the best way to handle this situation he had created was, but he was sure that bringing Meadow into his home was a mistake he might not be able to keep his hands off.

* * * * *

6:45 A.M.

"This is it?" Meadow asked as Abe parked the car in front of a huge stone building. Beautiful gardens surrounded it, and with the fairy lights strung up everywhere it looked magical. She could imagine that it would look like a winter wonderland when the whole landscape was covered with snow.

"It is," Abe replied.

"It's beautiful," she gushed. The whole town of River's End was just preciously adorable. Since it was light out—thin, watery dawn light but light nonetheless—she had been able to see the main street as they drove down it. There was an antique store, a jewelry store, an art studio, bookstore, ice cream parlor, clothing store, general store, toy store, and a store that looked like it sold outdoorsy things. All the stores were so cute with pretty hand-carved doors and signs hanging over them, awnings in different colors, and she was sure in the spring and summer there would be baskets of flowers everywhere.

The town was darling, and although when she had snuck down the stairs at Abe's house this morning she had intended to leave, now she was wondering whether she should stay here. Sooner or later she had always been going to have to stop running, maybe this was the right place to put down roots. River's End was pretty, and if Abe and Penny the waitress were anything to go by then the people here were lovely and kind, and if she had to live someplace, then she wasn't sure she could find a better place than right here.

And this place was small.

No one would ever think to look for her here.

Which meant she might just be safe.

It seemed like it was too much to hope for and yet she *was* hoping that she would be safe here.

She was having a baby, and even though she wasn't sure that she was going to keep it, she already loved it. If she decided to give it up it would be because it was what was best for her child, not because she didn't want it.

It was a part of her, but it was also a part of *him,* and there was no way he would give it up. So she would stay here, live with Abe, work here at this beautiful hotel, and try to build a new life. But if she thought he had managed to track her down then she would be out of here quicker than she could blink.

"Meadow."

She started, and her head snapped toward the voice to find that while she had been lost in thought, Abe had gotten out of the car, walked around it, opened her door for her, and was waiting for her to undo her seatbelt and get out. "Oh, sorry," she stammered, her fingers fumbling with the buckle as she tried to exit the car as quickly as possible. Abe had been so good to her, and she didn't want to disappoint him.

"Don't be sorry," he said, and his hazel eyes crinkled in annoyance.

Annoyance.

She hated being the cause of anyone's frustration.

It had been drilled into her that she must be perfect in every situation. She should know what people needed before they had to verbalize it and give it to them. She should be well dressed, hair and makeup done, standing quietly ready to serve, and that wasn't what she was doing right now.

She was failing.

"Meadow," Abe said again, grabbing her arm as she tried to hurry past him so he wouldn't see the tears threatening to cascade down her cheeks. "There's no need to be sorry about anything. You have a lot on your mind, I get that, it's okay to be distracted and worrying about what you and your baby's future looks like. You don't need to keep apologizing to me about everything."

"Okay," she agreed in a small voice. If it was what he wanted then she would try to do it.

Anything to make him happy.

He had done so much for her. Things that he didn't have to do. He hadn't had to buy her food at the diner, he hadn't had to invite her into his home so she wouldn't be sleeping on the street, and he didn't have to find her a job so that she could support herself and her baby. And yet he had.

How could she not want to repay him for that?

Abe was a good looking man. He had reddish-brown hair and a beard, which she'd never really found attractive before but thought suited Abe perfectly. He had tattoos on his arms, and from the looks of him he obviously worked out a lot.

She liked that.

It meant he was big and strong.

Someone who could take care of her.

And Meadow needed someone to take care of her.

Like he didn't believe that she would stop with the constant apologies anytime soon, Abe released her arm and started walking. "This way. I'll take you inside and introduce you to Maggie, and then I have to go to work."

While she didn't quite like the idea of him leaving her alone with a stranger she was glad that he'd be coming back for her later.

He *would* be coming back for her later, right?

He hadn't changed his mind?

"Abe?" she asked as she fell into step beside him. "Are you coming back to pick me up later?"

"Yes," he replied shortly.

Good.

Meadow gave an inward sigh of relief. Last night she had been unsure of her future, but Abe's cabin was cute, the bed had been the softest she'd ever slept on, and she had stood in his shower until the water ran cold because she had felt comfortable enough there. Right now she needed a place where she felt safe and secure, so she could finally learn what it meant to live her own life and not somebody else's.

Abe led her inside, and she wasn't surprised to see that the inside of the building was as beautiful as the outside. She was going to love working here, but ...

She was nervous as well.

She was twenty-four, but she hadn't had a job since she was in high school and that had just been babysitting. She didn't know anything about working in a restaurant. Meadow loved cooking, it was something she enjoyed and was good at, but this would be cooking for paying customers. What if they didn't like her food? What if she couldn't keep up? What if she let Abe down because she wasn't what his friend was looking for in a cook?

"Morning, Abe," a pretty brunette said as she walked toward them. The woman's hair hung in soft waves down her back, she had chocolate brown eyes, a warm smile, and a quietly confident air, Meadow liked her already.

"Morning, Maggie," he replied.

Maggie kissed his cheek then turned to her, smile still firmly in place. "You must be Meadow; I'm Maggie, a friend of Abe's. He said that you were a great cook and he knew I'd been looking for someone to help out here with the breakfast and lunch rush."

Abe had said that she was a great cook?

That was so sweet of him. She'd only cooked him one meal, just the vegetable pie last night. How had he picked up on her enjoyment for cooking from just that one moment?

Shy now and self-conscious as she worried about whether her

skills would measure up to what Maggie was looking for, Meadow gave a small smile and then hovered anxiously from foot to foot. It was overwhelming to be around people again, it wasn't the world she had lived in for so long, and she didn't just have to be around them she had to work with them.

This was too much.

Meadow very may well have turned and literally run out of here, but Abe nudged her shoulder.

Right.

He had told his friend that she could do this job therefore she *must* do this job.

No matter how many doubts and insecurities she had, she would have to ignore them and do this job to the best of her ability.

"Hi," she said to Maggie, "thank you for giving me this opportunity, I won't let you down, I promise."

"I'm not worried about that," Maggie said, waving it off. "The kitchen opened at six-thirty, but we're usually at our busiest by seven-thirty, so I'll show you the kitchen, get you up to speed as best as I can, and then you can get to work. After the breakfast rush quietens down we can talk about a more permanent arrangement, shifts and things, get you to fill out some paperwork before we get ready for lunch."

"See you later," Abe said.

"Bye," Maggie replied.

"Bye," Meadow echoed, wishing that he could stay. But he couldn't, he had a job to do, and so did she.

She would make him proud of her.

She had to, if she didn't he might send her away and she needed him.

* * * * *

12:08 P.M.

"You got someplace else to be?"

Abe looked up, only half paying attention to what his cousin Julian had just said, his mind was stuck elsewhere today, and he was having trouble concentrating. "Huh?"

"I said, you got someplace else to be?" Julian repeated with exaggerated patience.

"No. Why?"

"Because you're looking at your watch every five seconds," Julian replied.

"Just a little distracted I guess," he replied vaguely. He didn't want to get into a discussion right now on the cause of that distraction. This was a small town, gossip central, and his family was close with his father's brother's family, so he knew that it was only a matter of time before Julian, his brothers, and all of River's End knew that he had a houseguest. Still he wanted to delay the inevitable for as long as possible.

"Oh, and why is that?" Julian asked, his hazel eyes twinkling merrily.

Abe groaned. "You know. How?"

"You called Aunt Tatiana asking about whether Dahlia left any clothes behind. She must have called Mrs. Henderson to find out what she had in stock at the boutique, she must have spoken with Mrs. DuVall because the art studio is right next to the boutique, who must have spoken with Mr. Caputto who always rides his bike down Main Street on his way to have breakfast at the hotel ever since his wife died last spring. He talked to Maggie who mentioned having a new employee to Fletcher when he stopped by to speak with the couple who were mugged early this morning, and Fletcher told me when he came in." Julian was beaming like a kid on Christmas morning by the time he finished with his story.

Abe groaned again. Sometimes he really hated small-town life. You couldn't do anything without it spreading like wildfire.

"So I'm guessing this has something to do with the noise

outside the art gallery last night," Julian continued. "Since you were vague in your text last night telling me it was nothing to worry about I'm assuming that this mystery woman you're trying to keep under wraps is the noise in question."

There was no point in trying to hide anything, the whole town would be talking about it by sunset, and it wasn't like he was hiding Meadow away. She was working at the hotel, anyone who went there today would see her. "Her name is Meadow Smith."

"Is she pretty?" his cousin teased.

"Yes," he answered a little hesitantly.

"And she's not a criminal or a psycho?"

"Of course not."

"Well, from the way you're constantly checking the time, I'm guessing it's because you can't wait to get back to her. So what's the problem? Why did you sound all weird when you said she was pretty?"

"Because I think she's in trouble."

"Like the kind of trouble we deal in?"

"Yes."

"Then help her out of trouble so there's nothing standing in the way, then you can ask her out."

Julian made it sound so simple.

Find out what had Meadow on the run, fix it, and then ask her out.

But it wasn't that simple.

Meadow was pregnant, she saw him as her savior, and he wasn't marriage material or savior material.

That spelled disaster.

And there was no way he was going to do that to Meadow.

"She's pregnant," he told Julian.

"Are you worried about the baby's father coming back for her and his kid?" Julian asked.

"No. I'm worried that the baby's father is the reason she's on the run and sleeping behind dumpsters."

"You think whoever got her pregnant is dangerous?"

"I can't think of any other reason she would be homeless at five months pregnant."

"Can't argue with that," Julian said, looking thoughtful now. "Has she told you anything about him?"

"She hasn't told me anything at all besides her name and her age."

"Did you try running her name through the systems, see if it pops on anything?"

Abe just arched a brow. "I did that last night while she was sleeping. I didn't get any hits."

"If she won't talk and you haven't got hits in any databases then how are you going to find out what's going on with her?" Julian asked.

Now that he didn't have an answer to.

Yet.

But he *would* find a way to get the answers he wanted. He could be like a dog with a bone once he set his mind to something and ever since he'd found Meadow sleeping in that alley, his mind had been permanently stuck on her.

"They didn't get a good look at him," Fletcher Harris said as he breezed into his office. Fletcher was a few years younger than him and had been his youngest brother, Theo's best friend ever since they were kids.

"The mugging case?" he asked, trying to push thoughts of Meadow out of the forefront of his mind so he could do his job.

"Yeah, that's eight hits now, and we still don't have anything on him," Fletcher said, flopping down into the other chair at his desk. "And he's starting to escalate. He didn't hurt them badly, but he did rough them up a little, that's the first time he's done that."

Just as he had suspected their mugger was progressing, no longer was he content with just holding unsuspecting tourists up at knifepoint to steal whatever cash they had on them. Now he had roughed a couple up, throwing them up against a wall, giving the man a black eye. How long before he got tired of that too? How long before he used the knife not just as a tool to scare his victims but to stab someone with? How long before he killed someone?

"You know what I was thinking?" Fletcher said thoughtfully.

"No, what?" Julian asked.

"So far, he's only gone after tourists, no residents of the town have been mugged. I think that means that he's a local," Fletcher said.

The idea had occurred to him too, but this case was Fletcher's and he didn't want to step on his toes. Besides, he was confident that his deputy would figure things out on his own. He only hired people he trusted, and Fletcher had been practically a part of the family since they were kids, and he had served in the military beside his brother.

"You got someone specific in mind?" Abe asked.

"One person," Fletcher replied, his blue eyes razor-sharp. "Dylan Rodriquez lost his job last summer, he had to move back in with his parents, his wife left him, took the kids, and since he lost his job and he can't pay child support she's not letting him see the kids."

"Broke, lost his family, has to live with the parents, could lead him to need the cash and an outlet for his anger," Julian agreed.

He agreed as well. They needed a place to start, and Dylan Rodriquez was as good a place as any. "Why don't you start looking into him, ask around, see if he has alibis for any of the muggings and go from there."

"On it." Fletcher nodded, standing all energized and ready to end this case before anyone got seriously hurt. Fletcher paused at the door. "Oh, Abe, I forgot to ask. Is she pretty?" he asked, his blue eyes twinkling.

"Yes, now get out of here," he said gruffly. He was trying to keep his mind off Meadow, but it seemed like both his deputies were determined to play matchmaker and try to set him up even though it was the last thing he wanted.

Fletcher chuckled and headed out of the room, Julian was smirking, and Abe was about to ask about the case his cousin was working on when his phone rang. One glance at the screen and his mind was right back to Meadow.

"I have to take this."

"Sure," Julian said as he followed Fletcher out of his office.

He picked up his phone and pressed answer. "Levi, you got my messages," he said to his younger brother.

"No way I could miss them you left me like thirty," Levi shot back.

"It was two," he said. "And it was important."

"Yeah I got that," Levi said, and he could hear the smile in his brother's voice. "So what's so important? Does this have something to do with your guest?"

Did everyone know about Meadow? "How did you find out?"

"Mom. I stopped by with some fresh fish I caught when I went ice fishing yesterday, and she said you had called to ask if Dahlia left any clothes behind when she left. So what's up with your guest?"

"I was wondering if you could stop by tonight and take a look at her."

"Is she sick?"

"She's pregnant. She said five months, and I'm worried that whoever got her pregnant was also abusing her and that's why she ran. I was hoping you could check her out, make sure everything is okay with the baby, and also maybe see if she has any scars or anything that might give me some clues to what happened to her."

"You know if she tells me anything in confidence I can't tell you," Levi warned. "You want me to do this then I'll be her doctor and confidentiality comes into play."

He knew that, and he knew he had no right to ask his brother to break his oath, and yet he was desperate, he didn't know what else to do. Meadow needed help, and he was determined to give it to her.

* * * * *

5:26 P.M.

Meadow stared at the grandfather clock in the corner of the room.

It was nearly half-past five.

Abe was supposed to be here at five.

He wasn't coming.

She was sure of it.

He'd decided that no one in their right mind wanted to deal with a homeless pregnant woman who was on the run from a sadistic sociopath.

Of course he was going to get out as quickly as he could.

The worst part was she couldn't even blame him.

If their positions were reversed, she probably would have bolted as well. She was surprised he had stuck it out this long. Maybe he thought since he had gotten her a job that he had done his part, fulfilled his role as sheriff of River's End, and now he could walk away without feeling like he had turned his back on someone in need.

She was on her own again.

No, not again, she had *always* been on her own, and she always *would* be.

Meadow didn't know why she couldn't seem to accept that.

It wasn't like life hadn't told her that repeatedly.

Oh wait, it had.

Over and over again, apparently she was a slow learner and couldn't seem to get the message.

Loneliness was her curse to bear, and she'd better figure out a way to deal with it.

"Abe just pulled up outside, Meadow," Maggie stuck her head into the living room and called out.

Abe.

He was here?

He hadn't abandoned her?

With probably more enthusiasm than was strictly necessary, Meadow bounded out of her chair and hurried through the grand living room of Maggie's hotel, through the dining room and then the kitchen, then she stepped outside into the cold winter evening.

"Abe." She smiled up at him.

"Miss me, sunshine?"

"Yes," she answered honestly because she saw no reason to lie. Her answer obviously wasn't what he was expecting, and he shifted uncomfortably. Abe didn't like praise, she hadn't even known him for twenty-four hours and yet she already knew that about him. She wondered why. What had happened to him that had made his heart so carefully guarded? She had been through more than enough to have her heart close its doors, lock them, and then throw away the key, but it hadn't. She wanted love, she craved it, for Abe to have turned his back on the idea something bad must have happened to him.

"Yes, well, I'm here now," he said gruffly, already turning and heading back toward his truck.

"Were you working a case?" she asked, trailing after him. Meadow was intrigued by Abe's job, while she liked him, and she liked how he made her feel safe, she wasn't so stupid that she was going to blindly trust the first man she saw. She would wait a while, feel him out, get to know him, and then—maybe—if he turned out to be a good guy she might tell him what had happened to her and see if he could help her.

"Actually, we were," he said as he climbed into the driver's seat.

"What was it?" she asked, climbing in beside him.

"We've had several muggings here in town, someone targeting tourists, I'd been concerned that sooner or later the guy would progress from mugging to assault, and last night he took the first step toward that."

"Did he hurt someone?" She had thought that River's End would be a quiet, peaceful place to build a life for her and her baby but it sounded like maybe it wasn't. She knew that no place was perfect, and that any city or town, no matter how small, was bound to have crime, but still it made her feel uncomfortable.

"Not badly, and one of my deputies who was working the case interviewed a suspect today, and it turns out the guy is guilty."

"So you got him," she said with a smile, relaxing into her seat and looking out the window at the trees as they passed them by. She should have known that Abe wouldn't let some criminal wander around his town.

"Well, Fletcher did," he corrected, but it wasn't a correction she needed. Abe was the sheriff, and she was sure he had played a part in apprehending this mugger.

"It's so beautiful out here." Tall trees loomed above them, some had slender branches, devoid of leaves, that seemed to glimmer in the moonlight, others were fir trees and their green boughs made the forest look so black. But not a scary black, she liked it out here, she'd never really spent much time outside the city, but she thought she would like living in this quaint little town.

"It is," Abe agreed, and she heard a tranquility in his voice that she hadn't heard before. He loved this place too. It was like a little piece of paradise, and she couldn't wait to see it turned into a magical wintery wonderland when the snow came. There was just something about the snow that seemed to make everything beautiful. At least when the snow was fresh, then after a few days it just turned to gray, mushy slush, but before then it was perfect.

"How long have you lived in River's End?"

"My family moved here when I was eight."

"Who's in your family?"

"I'm the oldest, and I have three younger siblings, Levi is two years younger than me, then Theo is two years younger than him, and our sister Dahlia is the baby of the family."

"I bet she hated being a teenager with three older brothers," she said with a smile, imaging how Abe and his brothers must have scared off any boy who wanted to date their little sister.

"I'm ten years older than Dahlia. By the time she was a teenager, I was already out of the house," Abe replied.

"I bet no matter where you were any guy would have been scared of your wrath if he hurt your baby sister," she said.

Abe mustered a half-smile. "There may have been a few warnings issued," he said as he turned the car into his driveway.

Immediately she noticed that they weren't alone.

There was a car already parked up near the cabin.

"Someone is here," she said, wanting to hide the panic that she knew was written all over her voice and her face but knowing it would be impossible.

"It's okay, it's only one of my brothers," Abe assured her.

One of his brothers?

Why was one of his brothers here?

It wasn't that she was necessarily opposed to meeting new people, she had spent the day working at the hotel. But that had been different, Maggie didn't have a large staff, and she hadn't had to leave the kitchen to serve any of the guests, just cook in the relative quiet and safety of the pretty little kitchen.

Here she wasn't in a busy hotel, here she was alone in the woods with two men. She liked Abe, she trusted him, but she didn't know him, and she had been burned—badly—before, her skills at reading people were definitely lacking, and for a moment she wondered if she was once again going to offer herself up on a silver platter to a sick, evil man.

"It'll be fine, you'll like Levi," Abe assured her as he got out of the car.

As she had known he would, he walked around and opened her door for her. She climbed out, but she was no longer as happy to be back here as she had thought she would be when she'd been thinking of the cabin throughout the day. She'd thought she and Abe would have dinner, maybe sit by the fireplace for a bit, then she'd take a long, hot bath and go to bed, but now they had a guest.

Battling her instincts which were telling her to run and keep on running and never stop, Meadow followed Abe up the porch steps and through the front door where they were greeted by a man with dark hair and hazel eyes.

"Hey, Abe," the man—Levi—greeted his brother, then he turned to her. "I'm Abe's brother, Levi, you must be Meadow."

He held out his hand, and she reluctantly took it and shook it, but she didn't say anything.

"Levi's here to check you out," Abe told her.

Check her out?

What did that mean?

"Since I wasn't sure what led to you being homeless, I wasn't sure if you've been going to regular check-ups to monitor your pregnancy," Abe continued. "Levi is a doctor, he's going to give you a look over, just make sure that everything is okay."

A doctor.

Levi was a doctor.

She did *not* do well with doctors.

And Levi was a stranger.

There was no way she was letting this man anywhere near her.

When Levi reached out she darted backward, crashing into the now closed front door. "Don't touch me," she shrieked, possibly sounding just a tad bit hysterical. Without waiting to see what either Abe or Levi were going to do, she shoved past them and ran up the stairs. She went into the room she'd slept in last night and straight into the bathroom, where she locked the door behind her.

Meadow was breathing hard, her heart hammering in her chest as though she'd run a marathon instead of up one flight of stairs.

Scared and confused, she slid down the door and rested against it.

She didn't know what to do.

Just when it felt like she was starting to get her footing it was like the world was shaken beneath her again, leaving her all jumbled up.

She put a trembling hand on her stomach and felt her baby kick its tiny feet. She felt so guilty. Was she hurting this little baby by not letting Abe's brother give her a check-up? Was her emotional instability hurting her baby? How could she feel like the world's worst mother when her baby wasn't even born yet?

* * * * *

5:49 P.M.

"I wasn't expecting that," Abe said as Meadow fled up the stairs. "Sorry, Levi, if I'd known that having you here was going to upset her then I would have waited, talked to her first, and then called you to come over."

"It's okay," Levi assured him. "Given that we suspect she's a victim of abuse we probably should have expected that kind of reaction."

His brother was right.

He *should* have expected that bringing a stranger here without warning her first and then just telling her that a doctor should check her out wasn't going to go down well. Meadow was obviously on the run, which meant she was hiding from someone, whether that be a father, boyfriend, husband, friend, family member, or acquaintance, so having someone just show up, unannounced, at a place that she felt safe must have been a shock to her.

"I'll go see if I can get her to come down, I might have gone about this the wrong way, but I still think that she and her baby need to be looked at by a doctor." He was worried about Meadow, he didn't know how long she had been running, he didn't know how much she had been eating the last few days, weeks, or months, and if she hadn't been eating enough he was sure that would have affected her baby. He didn't know what had happened to her to cause her to run, there might be injuries that they didn't know about, and he just wanted to make sure that she and her baby were okay.

"Don't push her too hard," Levi warned. "It's obvious that she feels safe here with you, I think that's the most important thing right now. If you want her to open up to you then just talk to her, get to know her, let her get to know you, and then maybe once she does you'll have earned her trust enough that she'll tell you who she's running from and why."

That was good advice.

And something he needed to keep in mind.

Levi was right, Meadow did seem to feel safe with him, maybe he could take advantage of that to find out what had happened to her.

Abe knew how that sounded, and it wasn't like he wanted to take advantage of her in a bad way, but he was a cop, it was his job to protect people, especially those who were vulnerable, and right now Meadow was about as vulnerable as it was possible to be.

Taking the stairs three at a time, he assumed she had gone into the spare bedroom, and since the door was open and he couldn't see her, he had to assume that she was in the bathroom. He had enlisted as soon as he turned eighteen, done six years before returning home, by then his little sister had been fourteen, nearly fifteen, and from what he remembered, whenever she had an emotional outburst, she would lock herself in the bathroom, he hadn't known how to deal with that, and he had no idea how to deal with Meadow now.

Feeling more out of his element than he had in his life, Abe walked through the bedroom and rapped on the bathroom door. He might not know what he was doing, but he knew enough not to try to open the door, even if it wasn't locked she'd closed it for a reason.

"Meadow?" he called out, trying to listen to see if he could hear crying. In his years in law enforcement, he had dealt with his share of weeping victims and their families, but it never got any easier. He didn't think he would ever be comfortable around crying people.

There was no answer.

He knew that she could hear him so he said, "I'm sorry, I shouldn't have sprung this on you, I was just concerned, and my brother is only here to help. I'm not going to push you to let him give you a check-up, it's your body and your choice, but he's going to be here for the next hour, so if you change your mind you can come downstairs. If you want to come down anyway, have some dinner, watch TV, you can, and you can just tell us that you don't want to talk to Levi."

Again there was no answer.

Pressing his ear to the door, he strained to hear through the thick oak, Abe thought that he could hear crying, but he couldn't be sure.

"Meadow, you can talk to me. I know that something is going on with you, whatever happened to make you run away, you can tell me, I'm the sheriff, I might be able to help."

Silence.

She needed space, he got that.

"I'm here when you're ready to talk," he told her as he retreated back downstairs. Levi was right, there was no use pushing her too hard, it was only going to be counter-productive.

"You get anywhere?" Levi asked when he entered the kitchen.

"Nope. She's in the bathroom, she wouldn't come out, I told

her that you would be here for the next hour if she changed her mind. Is that okay?"

"Of course." Levi nodded as he started peeling carrots. "I'm making soup."

"That vegetable soup that you're obsessed with?" he asked with a curl of his lip. He much preferred meat over vegetables, but his brother was always on some health kick, and most of them involved cutting meat out of his diet.

"I can throw a little chicken in if you're going to complain," Levi shot back with a grin.

Growing up, he'd been close with his brothers, they'd been thick as thieves, and since their cousins, Julian and Will had always lived close by, it had been like having two more brothers. He'd always felt sorry that there was an age gap between Theo and Dahlia because they'd been so much older and hadn't been interested in hanging out with a little girl, so a lot of the time she had almost been like an only child.

Abe wondered what Meadow's childhood had been like. Had she had good parents like he had? Did she have any siblings? Did she have aunts, or uncles, or cousins who cared about her and were wondering where she was and if she was all right?

"Thinking about her?" Levi asked, his face serious.

"Did you see her arm when she put her hand out to shake yours?" he asked. Meadow was still wearing the same clothes she'd been in when he saw her in the diner, but his mom had dropped off a few of Dahlia's things for her. When she had shaken Levi's hand downstairs in the living room the hem of her sleeve had moved up a bit, and he'd seen scars. At least that's what he thought they were.

"Looked like there were some old scars," Levi said, confirming his suspicions.

"She was abused," he said grimly. Although he had suspected as much, having it confirmed still sucked.

"You think it was from whoever raised her or whoever got her pregnant?"

"Who's to say they're different people?" While he hoped that incest wasn't what had led to Meadow's pregnancy, she hadn't told him anything so he was working blind.

"You really think that?" Levi looked repulsed and furious by the notion.

"I don't know. There's a chance that the scars were from an accident or surgery, or they were self-inflicted."

"But you don't think so."

"No," he said slowly. His gut told him that Meadow was a victim of abuse, and that the pregnancy was related to that abuse. Which meant that her abuser was out there somewhere and if there was one thing he knew about abusers it was that they didn't like to let go of their victims. They saw them as possessions, possessions they didn't like to share, they were controlling, and there was no way that whoever had hurt Meadow and gotten her pregnant was going to just let her go and build a new life somewhere else, without her.

The man would come for her.

Sooner or later he would manage to track her down.

"You think she's in danger," Levi said.

"Oh, I know she is."

"How are you going to protect her?"

How, indeed?

Abe had no idea.

He didn't know anything about this man so he didn't know how to prepare for his inevitable arrival. If he had a name he would track him down, call the police in whatever city he lived in, and have him arrested.

One thing he did know was that this man couldn't have Meadow back.

She had fought for her freedom, and she and her baby deserved a chance at a normal life, and he was determined to make sure they got it.

* * * * *

11:33 P.M.

It had been six hours since she had locked herself in the bathroom, that should be long enough. Abe had told her that his brother was going to stay for an hour if she changed her mind and decided she would like a doctor to check her out, so he should be long gone, and it wasn't far from midnight so surely Abe would have gone to bed by now.

Slowly, partly because she felt like she had been drained of energy and partly because her body had stiffened up sitting on the hard tiles for the last six hours, Meadow stood and stepped over to the vanity. Turning on the tap, she waited until the water heated up, then ran a towel underneath it and used it to scrub her face, washing away the tearstains she knew were there. She was embarrassed about her hysterical outburst, and part of her wanted to make a run for it so she wouldn't have to face Abe.

Drying off her face, Meadow unlocked the door and cracked it open, half expecting Abe to be standing there waiting for her, or lounging on the bed, or sitting in the armchair in the corner. But he wasn't. The room was empty and the cabin was quiet, he really must have gone to bed.

Although she didn't want to admit it she was disappointed.

Maybe she just needed someone to care about her right now. She had only known Abe for twenty-four hours, that wasn't enough time for them to even have formed a friendship, but she thought that he cared about her. Even though she knew it was only in a he was the sheriff and she needed help kind of way, it was better than nothing. She hadn't even had that in her life so it was definitely a step in the right direction.

Creeping, because she didn't want to wake Abe, she tiptoed down the stairs and toward the kitchen. She was hungry, and Abe had told her that she should feel at home here and could use his home as she would her own, so she would fix herself some dinner and then try to go to sleep.

As she stepped through the kitchen door, she was lost in thought thinking about how if Abe knew what the houses she had lived in had been like he wouldn't have used that analogy, when she saw a moving shadow.

She screamed.

He was here, he'd somehow managed to track her down, and he was here to take her back with him.

Meadow probably would have turned and bolted, but light suddenly flooded the room and Abe appeared before her.

Abe.

It was only Abe.

She was so relieved her knees buckled and she wobbled.

Abe snapped his hands around her arms and steadied her. "It's only me," he said as though she might not have registered that yet. "I was waiting for you to come down, I wanted to make sure you were okay."

How lucky was she that the man who had found her and decided to help her was this sweet? "I thought you had gone to bed."

"You mean you *hoped* I'd gone to bed, am I right, sunshine?" he asked, raising an eyebrow as he released his hold on her.

"I suppose," she replied with a smile. While she *had* been waiting in the bathroom for him to go to bed, as soon as she had crept out she'd realized that actually she didn't want to be alone right now.

"Are you hungry?"

"Starving."

"My brother made soup," he said, going to the table and holding up a bowl.

She couldn't quite help a nervous shudder at the mention of his brother. She felt bad for being rude and running away when

Levi had only come here to be helpful, she hoped he wouldn't hold it against her. It hadn't been personal, just a bad experience with a doctor in the past that she knew shouldn't overshadow all doctors, but she hadn't been able to stop the visceral reaction.

"I'm sorry, Meadow, I shouldn't have sprung that on you. I should have spoken with you about it and then taken you to see Levi in the morning if you agreed," Abe spoke up.

"It's okay," she assured him. "It was a nice gesture, and I'm sorry I didn't react very well. Is your brother mad at me?" Years of conditioning had trained her to want to make others happy, no matter the cost to herself, and she was genuinely worried that she had hurt Abe's brother's feelings.

"He's fine. He understands, we both do, you ran because you were afraid of someone, someone who hurt you, probably the same person who fathered your baby, but I know you're not ready to talk about it yet. When you are, you know right where to find me."

His direct approach took away some of the panic that threatened to smother her as memories of why she had run attempted to shove their way to the front of her mind.

"Why don't we eat our soup in the living room? There's still a fire in the fireplace, and it's more comfortable in there," Abe suggested, carrying two bowls as he walked past her.

Meadow followed him across the hall and into the living room, it was cozy in here with the fire crackling, and she took the bowl Abe handed her and dropped down into one of the rocking chairs that sat in front of the fireplace.

Abe joined her, and they ate in silence, her eyes roaming the room and looking at the family photos that hung on the walls. There were old ones from when he was a kid, standing with a woman with wild red hair who was no doubt his mother, and a serious man with dark hair. She could pick out Levi which meant the youngest boy had to be the other brother, Theo, and as time progressed a little girl who was the spitting image of her mother appeared in the pictures.

Then her gaze fell on pictures of an older Abe in military uniform. "You were in the army?"

"I was, my father and both of my brothers as well."

Her hand found her pocket and curled around the box inside. "My dad was in the army, he died, stepped on an IED. He deployed when I was just a couple of months old so I never knew him, but I have his dog tags, I carry them with me everywhere I go."

"I'm sorry," Abe said, and she could feel the heaviness coating his words. He had no doubt lost friends the same way.

"My mom decided that she didn't want to raise a baby on her own, maybe I was a reminder of the husband she had lost, so she gave me up. I grew up in the foster care system," she told him, not quite sure why she was telling him all of this, maybe it was because she knew that in part he understood the loss she had endured.

"That's rough," he said, and again his words were heavy with emotion, and while she sensed that it had something to do with him and not just her and her lonely childhood, she didn't ask him about it.

"Thank you for serving our country, for making it a safer place for me and everyone else," she said, and she meant it. Those were words that she wished she had been able to say to her father, he had made the ultimate sacrifice for her and she hated that she hadn't lived a life to honor that sacrifice.

"It was nothing." He waved off her words.

"No, it wasn't," she said fiercely. "You gave up your life here to go and fight in another country, knowing that you might never come home, for people that you don't even know, that isn't nothing."

He offered her a one-sided smile. "Then I accept your thanks. I'm sorry, Meadow, I really am, I can't imagine growing up without parents, and to know that your mom chose to give you up, that's really rough."

"All I ever wanted was someone to love me. My dad was gone, my mom obviously didn't care about me, I had friends but it wasn't the same, my whole life I've been searching for that one person who'll wake me up every morning with a kiss, who'll hold me in their arms each night when we go to sleep, who thinks I'm the light of their life, who would say something silly just to make me laugh, and wipe away my tears. I thought I had found it once before, but ... but now I don't think that person is out there anywhere." Tears were brimming in her eyes, and she realized that she had very nearly spilled everything. Jumping to her feet, she thrust the bowl of soup into Abe's hands. "I'm going to bed."

With that, she rushed up the stairs for the second time tonight, only this time instead of seeking refuge in the bathroom, she flung herself down onto the bed. Her tears flowed, and she wondered what was wrong with her that nobody loved her.

She had tried so hard to find love and yet she always failed.

It had to be her.

There was something wrong with her, something that made her unlovable. She was no doubt destined to spend her life alone.

FEBRUARY 5TH

6:22 A.M.

Abe rolled over in bed, still half asleep, but when he caught sight of the glowing red numbers and saw it was nearly half-past six his mind snapped wide awake. He was surprised he had slept for five straight hours. He'd waited up for a while after Meadow went running upstairs in case she came back down and needed to talk. When an hour passed without a sign of her, he'd put the fire out and come upstairs, pausing at her bedroom door where he had heard the soft sound of her snoring, and gone to bed. He'd expected to lie awake for hours, but he must have been more tired than he'd thought because he didn't remember lying awake at all, he must have passed out as soon as his head hit the pillow.

As he climbed out of bed, grabbed a clean pair of jeans and white shirt from the closet, and headed into his bathroom to take a quick shower, he wondered what he would find when he went downstairs.

Was Meadow still here?

Had she fled during the night?

Although she had opened up to him a little last night, he knew that it would only take one little push to send her running straight back onto the streets.

If she ran he'd actually miss her.

He was surprised to realize that, but in the last thirty-six hours or so he had grown accustomed to her presence. She was mixed up, and yet there was a sweetness, an innocence about her that

65

was intriguing. It was like whatever she had been through had left cracks in her soul, but it hadn't shattered it. She was sweet, and she obviously hadn't given up on humanity because she had been able to trust him even though she had no reason to.

It made him want to find who had hurt her even more.

Who could take something so good and try to destroy it?

He had been in love once, and he had thought that she was the most precious gift he had ever been given. He would have walked through fire for her, he would have given his life in a second to keep her safe, he would have spent his entire life doing anything it took to put a smile on her beautiful face.

But it hadn't been enough.

She'd left, and she'd taken with her his faith in love and relationships. It had left him too jaded to bother giving romance a second try, and despite the wonderful example his parents had given him, he believed that the odds of finding your soul mate were equivalent to your odds of winning the lottery.

Seeing the twinkle in Meadow's eyes when she was excited and the sadness in her voice when she had talked about wanting to find a place to belong in the world and someone to love her, it had him thinking …

Thinking nothing, he told himself firmly as he shut off the water.

A little more anxious than he should have been to see if Meadow was still here, he quickly toweled off and threw on his clothes. He paused at the door to the spare bedroom and found it empty, the bed was made, and the curtains were opened, and for a second he thought that she had finally split.

Half wondering if it was worth jumping into his truck to drive around in the hopes of finding her, Abe was just convincing himself it was a waste of time because she could have been gone for hours already when he stepped into the kitchen.

Meadow was in there, she'd obviously found the clothes his mom had dropped off because she was wearing a pair of loose fitting blue sweatpants that matched her sky blue eyes, and a golden yellow sweater that reminded him of the sun as it was rising.

It was perfect for her.

"Morning, sunshine," he drawled, and watched amused as she jumped at the sound of his voice.

"You did that on purpose," she accused when she saw him standing there grinning at her.

"Who me?" he asked all innocent as he took a seat at the table. "I wasn't sure I was going to find you still here." The look on her face as she went back to what she'd been doing confirmed his suspicions that she was still unsure whether or not she was going to hang around. Abe knew that she felt safe in his house, and Maggie said that she seemed to have enjoyed working at the hotel, she obviously liked River's End, and he couldn't blame her, the town was charming, but she was afraid and fear could fuel you into making some unwise choices. As much as he wanted to force her to trust him and open up so he could help her, he knew that trust had to be earned, so he had to just keep doing what he was doing.

"I'm sorry for running out on you last night," she said.

"Pfft." He waved off her apology, he didn't want contrition he wanted her trust. "Did you sleep well?"

"Yes."

"And I see you found the clothes my mother dropped off for you. I know you need some maternity clothes but I thought that they might do until we can get you what you need."

"I did, and I can make them work for now, please thank her for me, and your sister too, it was very generous of her to let me use her clothes."

"I will, they look good on you."

She shot a quick glance his way, and her cheeks heated when she saw the appreciative look he was giving her. "I, umm, well, I need to be at the hotel by quarter to seven, so I need to leave soon," she said, changing the topic.

"I'll drop you off on my way to work," he told her. "I just need to grab a quick breakfast."

"I, uh, I made you breakfast," she said shyly, holding up something wrapped in white paper. "It's pancake wraps."

"Pancake wraps?"

"I make the pancakes a little bigger and then I put fruit or something on them and roll them up," she explained. "I made one with berries, one with apple and banana and added a little cinnamon, and one with Nutella and chocolate chips in case you like something sweeter."

"You're a gem," he told her.

Her cheeks pinked again. "I only want one. Which two do you want?"

"Whichever ones you don't."

"Oh." She looked surprised that what she wanted should matter. "I really don't mind."

Since he knew it wasn't her parents who had abused her, and combined with her admission that she had once thought she'd found someone to love her, he suspected that she was a battered wife who had finally had enough, probably when she found out she was pregnant. It made sense that she wasn't used to someone caring about her needs. Well, she was going to have to get used to it, because although he wasn't in the market for a wife, he knew how to treat any woman right, here she would learn that she deserved respect and maybe it would start to sink in after no doubt having it beaten out of her.

"Make up your mind, sunshine, because we have to leave. Grab your coat." Abe stood and grabbed his from the hook by the door, heading out to get the truck warming up.

By the time he had the engine running, Meadow had come out the front door, coat on, and the three pancake wraps in her hands. "Don't you need to lock the door?" she asked as she climbed into the passenger seat.

"Not in River's End," he replied. The notion looked so foreign to Meadow that he wondered whether her abusive ex had locked her up inside the house. "So did you decide which of the wraps you wanted?"

"Well, if you're sure you don't mind," she hedged.

"I don't."

"I love berries, so I wouldn't mind that one."

"Perfect, I love chocolate, and apples, especially with cinnamon. You should show these pancake wrap creations of yours to Maggie. I'm sure she'd love to offer them for breakfast at the hotel."

"Really?"

"Of course, they're a great idea, and perfect for people in a hurry."

"You really think they're a good idea?"

"Definitely. You're full of great ideas, Meadow, I'm sorry that someone made you feel like you're not, like you're worthless, but it's not true. Whoever told you those things, *they're* the one with the problem, not you. He made you believe things about yourself that aren't true because he wanted to control you, but he doesn't. You left. Even though part of you believed the things he told you, you left anyway because you didn't want your baby to have that life. That takes guts. Guts, and strength, and courage that prove that everything he told you about yourself is a lie."

Meadow was quiet for a moment, and then she lifted a hand and brushed at her eyes. "Thank you."

The words were simple and yet never in his life had he heard so much emotion expressed in two words. "You're welcome."

* * * * *

10:52 A.M.

"Why don't you take a break?"

The words filtered slowly through her brain like they had to pass through a maze to get there. Meadow had almost forgotten them by the time they did make it into her brain.

She was busy.

Preoccupied.

She was baking bread, and chopping tomatoes and cucumbers for the salad, and stirring soup that was bubbling away on the stove. Chicken was frying, and potatoes were boiling, and her mind was spinning in a million different directions as she prepared for the lunchtime rush.

A lot of organization went into cooking, making sure everything was timed down to the last second so that it was ready all at once, making sure everything was done just right but also as quickly as possible so that things didn't burn or overcook. Her brain was wired to work like this, it was why she had always loved to cook. Even as a child in a group home she would often cook dinner for herself and all the kids who lived there, it gave her a purpose, and …

Meadow was embarrassed to admit it, but she also hoped it would make people like her.

Hungry tummies led to warm hearts, right?

Back then, baking cookies and cupcakes and brownies to give to the other kids had earned her friendships, but over time she had learned that you couldn't buy people off. One by one those people had drifted out of her life, and no amount of chocolate was going to keep them there.

Still, that love of cooking hadn't faded, and when she had been alone in her house, day after day, she would spend the time cooking because she knew she was good at it, and more than once, it had saved her from a beating.

"Meadow." A hand rested lightly on her shoulder, and she very nearly jumped out of her skin, she had forgotten anyone else was even in the kitchen. "Why don't you take a break? You've been working nonstop since you got here."

Maggie was standing beside her, looking at her with anxious brown eyes coated with concern. Because she didn't want anyone to be worried about her, she pasted a smile on her face. "I don't really need a break."

"I disagree, and since I'm your boss I insist that you take a break. Do you like tea?"

Well, she didn't know what to say to that. Maggie had very generously given her a job here and she didn't want to do anything to upset her boss, so reluctantly she set down the knife that was in her hand and left the half chopped carrot on the cutting board. "I like tea."

"Good." Maggie nodded, satisfied. "Why don't you get some of the cookies you baked this morning, and we'll sit together, get to know each other a little better."

Obediently she collected some cookies, set them on a plate, and took them over to the small table in the corner of the kitchen. The morning rush had ended at ten, and the lunch rush wouldn't start till noon so although they had time for a quick rest she wanted to get back to work. Meadow was worried that if she messed up, if she didn't work hard enough or do everything perfectly that she would be out of a job. And if she was out of a job then she could hardly expect to stay in Abe's house for free, leaving her and her unborn baby out in the cold. Literally.

"You can stop fretting," Maggie said as she set two mugs of tea down on the table and dropped into the chair beside her. "You're the best employee I've ever had, by far. You have this job for as long as you want it which is why I thought we should get to know each other a little better."

Meadow raised a suspicious eyebrow. Was this an attempt to get her to talk about why she had been on the run?

"Relax," Maggie said with a small chuckle. "I just thought we might have some things in common."

"Things in common?" she echoed. She wasn't sure what she could possibly have in common with a beautiful, smart, successful business owner.

"I don't mean to pry, honestly I don't, I only want to help. You're running from someone, right? Someone who hurt you."

When she had run up the stairs and gone to bed last night she had been consumed with thoughts of *him*. All night he had plagued her dreams, taunting her, promising her that he would get her back. This morning when she had woken, the urge to run again and never stop was strong, but she owed it to her baby to give this a proper try, so she had put on her big girl panties, made breakfast and come to work, she wasn't going to let him take anything else from her. But this she hadn't been expecting. Had she really found someone who truly understood?

"You don't have to talk about it if you don't want to. I just thought that you might like having someone to talk to. I know how lonely it can be, and I can't imagine being pregnant and afraid like that, so …" Maggie trailed off, looking like maybe she shouldn't have brought it up.

"Thank you." She wished that she could offer an appropriate amount of thanks for the gratefulness that was inside her heart. Those two little words didn't feel like enough, not when she had said them to Abe this morning and not now. "Who hurt you?"

"Pretty typical stuff." Maggie shrugged. "Alcoholic Dad, drug addict Mom, I was lucky to get out, my grandparents took me in after my dad went to prison and life for me was better after that."

"How old were you?"

"Twelve."

"My dad died when I was a baby, my mom didn't want me so she gave me up. I know what it's like to be a kid and all alone. All I ever wanted was to find my place in the world, that place where you just … belong."

"I know that feeling." And from the look on Maggie's face she truly did.

"Do you think that everyone has a place? Do you think that for some people there isn't anywhere they belong? That they're destined to spend the rest of their lives alone and searching for something that doesn't exist?" That was her greatest fear, that she would forever be alone, trying to hunt for something that wasn't even there.

"I don't know," Maggie replied, and the wistful tone in her words said that she had the exact same fears.

It was rough not growing up in a real home, with people who loved and cared about you, people who helped you form the foundation for which your entire life would be built on. Meadow was about to ask Maggie more about what had happened to her in the hopes that it would make her feel more comfortable opening up when the door to the kitchen was flung open and Abe bustled through, striding purposefully toward them.

"Hey, Maggie. Sunshine." He nodded at each of them.

Every time he called her that it was like a little sliver of light crept into her dark world. She wondered what would happen if she let him all the way in. Would her whole world erupt into light like the sun rising at dawn? "Hi, Abe." She smiled shyly.

"What are you doing here in the middle of the day?" Maggie asked.

"We have a crime scene," Abe replied, and from the look in his hazel eyes it was a bad one. "I don't know what time I'm going to be back so I'm going to leave the car here so you can go home when you're finished your shift," he told her.

"Oh," she said. Disappointment flooded through her to know he wouldn't be picking her up and they wouldn't be spending the evening together. "Okay."

"The house is unlocked, make yourself at home. I don't know what time I'll be back tonight, it might be late. If you feel safer you can lock the doors when you go to bed. I have a key on me," he rattled off. "Are you going to be okay on your own?"

Was she going to be okay on her own?

What kind of question was that for someone who had been on their own for as long as they could remember?

She would be okay, and yet … she'd miss him.

It was silly, he would be home at some point, and when she ran it hadn't been expecting to find someone who would very quickly mean something to her. But she had. Abe could be everything she had ever wanted, but the truth was she still didn't really know him, and she wasn't going to make the same mistakes she had before.

So it was time to pull up her big girl panties again.

"I'll be fine," she assured Abe, and for some strange reason she actually believed it. Maybe the kind words he had spoken to her in the car this morning were starting to seep in. Maybe she was stronger than she gave herself credit for. Maybe it wasn't the be-all and end-all that she find someone to love her. Maybe she could be on her own and still be okay.

* * * * *

2:16 P.M.

Carla strained her ears.

Silence.

But was it real silence or a deceptive silence?

Sometimes when you tried really hard to listen out for sounds your mind created them out of thin air to confuse you.

She hated that.

It was like her own body was working against her, the betrayal stung almost more deeply than his had.

She strained some more, she was positive it was quiet. He was gone, but for how long? He could come back at any second, and if he found out what she was going to do, he was likely to beat her into a bloody pulp, killing her just because she wanted to cling to her life.

He would think it was funny.

Carla could imagine him standing over her dead body,

chuckling to himself that her will to live had caused her death.

Well, she wasn't going to give him that pleasure.

She wasn't going to give him *any* more pleasure.

She wasn't going to just sit here and wait for him to play with her until he got bored and then kill her. For all his talk of wanting to train her to make her just the way he wanted her to be, she didn't really see him lasting that long.

He wanted to take her life.

He wanted to claim her soul, and he was too angry to wait long to do it.

Carla had never seen a person as angry as him. He hid it well, she hadn't caught even a glimpse of it before she had willingly gone to him, but once he got her alone it had shone through so brightly it was blinding. His anger was like the sun, it burned your skin, it stole your sight if you looked at it, it made you want to shrivel in a ball, seeking any sort of shade you could just to hide from its strength.

Five days.

Had it really been only five days?

It felt like she had been his prisoner for a lifetime. She had certainly aged a lifetime in those five days.

But five days were enough.

When he had left earlier, he left her restrained, naked, her hands tied together and then to the bar above the bath where the shower curtain hung. He had filled the bath with ice water and left her to stand in it, thinking it would torture her.

And it would have.

If she was standing in it.

But she was a gymnast, her small stature and the hours of training she had put into it meant she was good. Good enough that she had been able to lift her body weight up and out of the water, now she balanced on the edge of the bath, and the extra height had allowed her to see her bound hands. It had taken much longer than she had hoped, but she had managed to get the ropes mostly untied.

Any moment now she was going to be free.

And there it was.

With one more tug, the rope came undone.

There was no time to waste, he could return at any second, and if he didn't find her standing with her feet in a bath filled with ice, he was going to be furious.

Between his beatings and whippings and the vicious way he had raped her, Carla was sore and stiff and moving was hard, but she wasn't stopping, not for anything. If she wanted her life then she was going to have to fight for it.

The clothes she had been wearing five days ago when she walked into the lion's den were long since gone, and he hadn't given her anything else to wear so she was going to have to run naked. Humiliation and embarrassment had no place in her current situation so she shoved them away. This was about saving her life, and right now, nothing else mattered.

Ever since the night he had taken her they had been traveling. She wasn't sure where and she didn't really care, all she wanted was out of this room. He kept her drugged, bound, gagged and blindfolded in the trunk of his car when they traveled. She guessed he didn't want to take any chances of her alerting anyone to her presence, so she had no idea where they were. She always woke up inside a cheap motel room.

From the way he made her scream the motel rooms he chose must be remote, so when she managed to stagger out of the small, dirty bathroom, and then through the small, dirty bedroom, she wasn't surprised to find nothing but forest surrounding her. Carla didn't care, there had to be people around someplace fairly close by so all she had to do was run.

She would gladly run for hours, naked, through the cold forest if it just meant that she found safety and the end of her journey.

Carla spun in a circle, trying to figure out which way was the best direction to go if she wanted to find someone quickly. She picked a direction at random when she couldn't figure out a better plan. She had never really been an outdoorsy girl, and the forest all looked the same to her.

Just as she started running she heard it.

The rev of a car engine.

He was back.

Sparing only a second to throw a glance over her shoulder to confirm that indeed her abductor had arrived and was climbing out of his car right this very second, she ran.

The thundering behind her said that he was following, and close on her tail.

She didn't stop, she didn't even slow. She was pumped so high on adrenalin that she didn't feel the sticks and stones that tore at her feet, or the branches that ripped at her hair and her skin as she darted around trees.

The footsteps got louder.

He was gaining on her.

She had barely eaten in five days, been drugged numerous times, raped and tortured, she was no match for him.

He was going to win.

Carla knew that and yet she didn't falter in her drive.

Drive had made her be the best gymnast she could be, it had led her to study hard and make grades good enough to get a college scholarship. Drive had helped her through everything she had ever done in her life and she wasn't giving up now, it wasn't in her nature.

Her abductor didn't say anything, he didn't yell at her to stop, he didn't threaten her, he just ran, and Carla took that to mean that they were close enough to people that he was worried about someone overhearing him.

People were around here somewhere, she was sure of it.

There.

Up ahead.

The trees were thinning out a little.

As she got closer she saw a building with a light on inside it. She could see the glow of it in the overcast day.

So close.

She was so close, but just as she thought she truly stood a chance at getting away he slammed into her, knocking them both to the ground.

The landing was hard, and his big body landing on top of her shoved the air from her lungs. Pain shot up through her wrists and knees, flooding her whole body until she was just one great big burning pile of agony.

"I didn't find that amusing," he growled in her ear. He was breathing hard, and she could feel his chest heaving, Carla took some satisfaction from the fact that she had made him work to take her life.

He flipped her around onto her back, pinning her down as he straddled her hips. Carla glared up at him defiantly, she was done begging, she was done trying to please him in the vain hope that he would let her go.

That wasn't happening.

If he was going to kill her, she would rather he hurry up and get it over and done with.

Somehow he must have sensed that because he nodded. "You're more trouble than you're worth, and easily replaceable," he sneered. "You want death so badly then you can have it." Standing, he dragged her up with him and then he yanked rope— which he seemed to have an unending supply of—from his pocket. He looped it around her neck in such a way that when he prodded her to start walking it pulled tight, strangling her if she got too far ahead of him.

He walked her back through the forest the way they had come, and now that she wasn't running for her life she noticed how beautiful it was out there. Carla wished she had spent more time out in nature, letting the beauty of the natural world inspire her.

It was too late now.

It was too late for a lot of things, but at least she knew her family would be proud of how hard she had fought. She was strong, not strong enough to defeat this evil man, but strong enough to know that he hadn't destroyed her.

It wasn't much, but it was something to take with her to whatever lay beyond this world.

* * * * *

4:25 P.M.

Meadow yawned.

It had to be the thousandth time today.

She was exhausted, too much stress these last few days, and too many horrors these last few years, and it felt like all at once it was catching up with her. She felt like she could lie down—anywhere—close her eyes and sleep for about a month.

A small delighted moan escaped her lips at the thought of it.

It had probably been five years since she had last had a good night's sleep, a night that hadn't been filled with fear and nightmares and the anxiety that she had done something wrong even though she was asleep and not in control of her actions.

Would that fear ever leave her?

It had been six days since she had run, and so far, that fear had only gotten worse. She kept expecting that at any second she would turn around and see him standing there.

Waiting for her.

Ready to grab her and drag her back to that house where she and her baby would be forced to stay the rest of their lives. Captives. *His* captives. Powerless to stop him from doing whatever he wanted to do to them.

Maybe with time things would improve. It hadn't even been a week yet, of course she was still on edge, anxious, twitchy, nervous. That was perfectly normal, but in time, maybe after months or years had passed that fear would fade, and she wouldn't have to live her life looking over her shoulder.

It was a nice thought but …

She wasn't sure that it would ever happen.

She had been with him for too long, his prisoner, his pet, his favorite toy, and his hold on her was probably too strong to ever be broken.

But it couldn't hurt to hope.

Another yawn caught her by surprise and the knife which she was using to dice tomatoes ready for tonight's dinner at the hotel slipped and nicked her finger. It wasn't deep, but it was deep enough to start bleeding, and she quickly hurried over to the sink, grabbing a piece of paper towel on the way.

"That's it, you're going home," Maggie announced, appearing behind her.

"What?" Meadow ran cold water over the cut and watched as the blood joined the water and dribbled down the sink.

"You've been standing here for hours yawning, and now you cut yourself. You're pregnant and exhausted and scared that whoever you're running from will track you down, you should go home, go to bed, try to sleep."

"I'm supposed to be here until five," she protested, turning the tap off and wrapping the paper towel around her finger.

"It's okay, we can cover you."

"You shouldn't have to cover for me, I've only been here two days, and besides I kind of need the money," she said, dipping her eyes in embarrassment.

Maggie waved off her concerns. "It's fine, it's only thirty minutes early, I won't dock your pay, and really we can cope without you."

"Are you sure?" As much as she didn't want to be lazy and a bad employee, especially when she had only been here for two days, and she was in desperate need of the cash, the idea of going back to Abe's, curling up in the bed in his spare bedroom, and just sleep was very appealing.

"Of course I'm sure. Stick a Band-Aid on that and then go home. I'll see you in the morning," Maggie said firmly.

Well, she couldn't argue with her boss. "Thank you."

Maggie smiled. "You're welcome."

By the time Meadow walked over to the first aid kit and grabbed a Band-Aid the cut had mostly stopped bleeding, so she quickly put it on, threw away the paper towel, and then went to the counter where she'd been working. She sterilized the knife, then the counter, and threw the tomatoes in the bin.

With a weary sigh, she grabbed her coat and purse and headed out the door. It had been a long time since she had driven a car, let alone a large truck, and she was a little anxious about driving Abe's back to his place. Since she didn't have a choice, she unlocked it, climbed in, and started the engine.

It roared to life, and she almost backed out and decided that she would just stay here until Abe was done with work and could pick her up, but she had already decided that this was a big girl panties kind of day, so she put both hands on the steering wheel and started driving.

Once she got going it wasn't so bad, and by the time she turned onto Main Street, she was actually feeling pretty pleased with herself. The street was busy today, buzzing with people, and since she had mostly driven along here early in the morning or later at night after most of the stores closed it was nice to see the place busy.

This really was the most adorable town, and if she had to stay somewhere she was glad she'd chosen here. The place was so small that she was sure it really wasn't possible for him to find her here; if she kept telling herself that then who knows, she might actually come to believe it at some point.

Leaving the main street, she headed up into the forest, it was only another mile and then she would be turning into Abe's driveway. She wondered if she could figure out how to light a fire.

It was cold and sitting beside the crackling wood, watching the flames dance about would be a nice way to fall asleep.

Meadow was distracted, and she didn't see the car coming in the opposite direction, aiming right for her, until it was almost upon her.

With a shriek she yanked hard on the wheel, sending Abe's truck skidding off the road and slamming into a tree.

The impact hit her hard.

Her chest yanked against the seatbelt as she was thrown forward, and her head hit the steering wheel with enough force for her to see stars.

He had found her.

She had no idea how that was even possible, but he had.

The truck that had almost run her off the road had pulled to a stop, and she could see someone climbing out.

He was coming for her.

He was going to throw her into his vehicle and drive off with her, and no one would ever see her alive again.

The man—dressed all in black but she knew who he was—was walking toward her.

Stalking would be a more appropriate word.

Stalking toward her with a pompous arrogance that said he was going to get what he wanted.

He *always* got what he wanted.

Meadow fought with her seatbelt, trying to get it undone with hands that were shaking too hard to be anything even remotely helpful.

She had to run.

She had to get away from him.

He was getting closer.

Then all of a sudden, another truck stopped in the street, voices spoke, and the man who had run her off the road turned and headed back for his truck. A second later its tires screeched and it took off down the road.

He was gone.

Gone.

Was she really that lucky?

Could he really have taken off?

"Miss?"

A face appeared beside her, and she shrieked.

What if he had sent someone to kidnap her?

"This is Abe's truck. Are you that girl he has staying with him? The one with the pretty name, Meadow, isn't it? I'm Darren Sutton. I live on the property next to Abe's. Are you okay?"

How did he know her?

Was he lying?

No, River's End was a small town, no doubt the gossip mills had already made sure that every resident in the vicinity knew about her.

"S-someone r-r-ran me o-off th-the r-r-road," she stuttered. Her heart was hammering so hard in her chest she was sure he must be able to see it. With each beat it sent knifing pain through her chest.

"That guy that took off when we got here?" Mr. Sutton asked.

"Y-yes."

"Hey, Bill, you get the license of the truck that just took off?" he called over his shoulder.

"Yeah, it fled the scene of an accident," Bill called back.

"It wasn't no accident," Mr. Sutton told him. "He ran Sheriff Abe's guest off the road. We'll call an ambulance, miss, get you to the hospital to get checked out."

No.

She wasn't going to any hospital.

She had to get to Abe's.

That was the only place she felt safe.

"No, no, it's okay, I'm okay," she said in a rush, finally managing to wrestle the seatbelt undone and stagger out of the car.

"Miss, I don't think that's a good idea," Mr. Sutton told her.

Right now she didn't care what he thought. Abe's house had to be only half a mile away, she just wanted to get there. She was pretty sure she wasn't hurt badly enough that she was going to pass out along the way.

Pushing past the man and his well-meaning hands that reached out to try to steady her as she stumbled, Meadow started walking.

* * * * *

5:13 P.M.

Abe reached out, and with a gloved hand opened the door of the car.

The first thing he noticed was the smell.

There was the coppery smell of blood that one would expect when a victim had been viciously sliced in half, but there was something else.

Something sweet, flowery, pretty.

"It smells like a meadow in here," Julian said, standing beside him.

He froze.

His heart clenched.

His cousin was right.

It *did* smell like a meadow in here.

"What did you just say?" he ground out through clenched teeth. Not because he was angry at his deputy, but because he didn't want his thoughts to be running in the direction they were currently moving.

"That it smells like a meadow in here," Julian repeated, his eyes growing wide as he realized what he'd just said. "Do you think …?"

"That this has something to do with Meadow?" Abe asked. He hoped it didn't, he *prayed* it didn't, but Meadow turned up here, clearly on the run, and then just a couple of days later they had two murders. The scene of one was full of flowers that made the car where the body had been left, smell like a meadow. "I hope it doesn't, but it seems like too big a coincidence to ignore."

"You think she killed this woman and left the flowers here?" Julian asked.

"No," he balked at the very notion. "She's at the hotel with Maggie where I dropped her off this morning. This woman has been dead a couple of hours, there's no way she could have gotten here and killed her. Besides, Meadow isn't strong enough, particularly five months pregnant, to lift the body and pose it like that."

"You think maybe she's working with a partner then?"

"No. Definitely not," he said firmly. "Levi and I both saw scars on her arms, and the fear in her eyes when I found her sleeping behind that dumpster that can't be faked."

"Then this killer is who she's running from," Julian stated the only logical conclusion they could form. If she wasn't working with this man then she was running from him.

"There's no way to know that this has anything to do with her," Abe said, but he knew that wasn't true. It had been over a year since there had been a murder in River's End and that was domestic violence. They had known who had committed it, and while that didn't make it any more pleasant at least it made sense. Since Meadow had arrived in town just days ago, there had been two murders. This poor woman who had been ripped open and left strung up in a car filled with flowers, and the man who had owned the car she had been left in who had been stabbed over a dozen times.

"You're right," Julian said, although his face said the opposite. "It could be a coincidence that Meadow turns up in River's End and then someone kills a guy to steal his truck, then kills a woman in it and leaves dozens of flowers along with the body."

"Abe, we got another incident."

Abe looked up at his other cousin Will, and frowned. After spending the last couple of hours at the scenes of two murders he didn't want any more bad news. "Another murder?"

"No." Will shook his head. "Attempted murder maybe, someone ran a car off the road and then disappeared when someone stopped to help."

What was with this sudden crime spree?

Did they have someone who had turned up in his sweet, peaceful little town to try to kill as many people as they could before they were stopped?

"Abe," Will said, and Abe didn't like the tone of his cousin's voice. "The truck that was run off the road was yours."

His?

Meadow.

If he'd had doubts that this murder was somehow related to her then they were gone now. Whoever had killed this woman must have managed to track Meadow down and attempted to get to her.

Lifting eyes that he was sure portrayed much more of the fear that was swirling inside him than they should have, he asked, "Is Meadow okay?"

"She was conscious at the scene and wouldn't let anyone help her. Apparently she went running off into the forest."

So she was gone?

If she had run, he doubted he would ever find her which meant she would be unprotected and ripe for this killer to pluck and take off with her.

"On a hunch that she would go to the one place she felt safe, Fletcher went to your place and she's there, she's locked in the bathroom upstairs, she won't open up and let him in, but he's staying there until you get there."

Will had raised a brow as though there was some doubt in his mind that Abe would leave and head straight home to check on Meadow.

There wasn't.

"You got this?" he asked Julian.

"Of course, I can handle things here. You go make sure Meadow is okay."

"I'll call you," he said, already scrambling in his pocket for the keys to the cruiser they had taken out here after he'd dropped off his car with Meadow. "Will, can you stay here as well please, Julian is going to need a ride back, and since I'm not staying I need both of you here."

"Sure thing," Will agreed.

Abe didn't remember the drive to his house. He was sure he smashed the speed limit, his sirens were screaming and his lights were flashing, practically yelling at anyone who came near him to get out of his way.

Thankfully, he made it home in one piece, and he was relieved to see Fletcher's car in the driveway. He was afraid that now that this man had killed someone, he would make his move on Meadow. She had managed to evade his earlier attempt, even if it wasn't because of anything she had specifically done, and he was sure that had made the killer angry.

That the two weren't related wasn't even a possibility as far as he was concerned.

"Fletcher," he called out as he flung his front door open.

Fletcher stepped out of the kitchen. "She's still up there."

"It might be better if you leave, she doesn't do well with strangers."

"Okay, good luck."

He nodded once and then took the stairs three at a time. "Meadow," he said as he hammered on the bathroom door. "It's Abe. I know what happened, and I know that you didn't hang around to be checked out by paramedics. Last time I didn't push you into opening the door, but tonight if you don't open this door in the next ten seconds, I *will* break it down. One," he started counting, he was deadly serious. She had been in a car accident, he needed to know if she was okay, and he needed to know who she was running from before he came for her again. "Two."

"Okay, okay," he heard her mumble from the other side of the door and a moment later it swung open.

Abe frowned when he saw her. There was blood on her head along with a lump the size of a golf ball. She had one arm pressed to her chest, and she was hunched over. It took every ounce of self-control he possessed to not sling her over his shoulder and drive her to the hospital.

"Why didn't you wait for the EMTs?" he forced out through clenched teeth.

Meadow just shrugged.

He grunted, then sighed, then reached out and gently took her elbow. "Let's go downstairs and patch you up."

She didn't fight him and leaned heavily against him as they slowly made their way back downstairs. Since she had managed to make her way back here on foot without passing out, Abe had to assume that her injuries weren't life-threatening, but she still didn't look good.

"I'm going to call my brother Levi who you met the other night," he said as he eased her down onto the couch. "I know you didn't want him to look at you then, but you were just in a car accident, and we need to know how badly you're hurt."

"No," she said. Her voice was firm, but when she shook her head he noticed her wince.

He tutted disapprovingly, but stood and left the room, gathering his first aid kit and a wet cloth. Returning to the living room, he sat beside her and took her chin between his thumb and forefinger, tilting her face so he could better see her wound. Meadow sucked in a breath, and he couldn't help but notice that her gaze had dropped to his lips.

Ignoring the sudden stirring in his pants, he dabbed at the blood that streaked her face. "Did you get a look at the car that ran you off the road?"

"No," Meadow replied softly.

He didn't believe her. "You know who he is, don't you?"

She didn't say anything.

"He killed two people, Meadow," he informed her as he released her and pulled some butterfly bandages from his kit. "He killed a man to steal his car, then he cut a woman virtually in half and strung her up in the stolen car. He filled the vehicle with flowers so it smelled like a meadow. A *meadow*," he repeated for emphasis. He knew she was afraid, but how could he help her if she wouldn't talk to him?

Still Meadow wouldn't speak.

Taking her chin again, he placed the small strips of white tape on the cut on her forehead. "You can trust me, Meadow. I want to help you. Is he your boyfriend? Husband? Is he the father of your baby? He followed you here, do you know how? I can't keep you safe if you won't talk to me."

Her eyes met his, and he could practically feel her fear, but she still wouldn't speak.

She just stared at him.

Silently, begging him to help her.

Lifting his thumb, he brushed it lightly across her bottom lip, and she sucked in a surprised breath.

"I should take your pulse," he said, his voice husky. He released her chin and picked up her wrist. When he pressed his fingertips to her soft skin he could feel it thumping wildly, but now he wasn't sure if it was because of the accident or the sudden sexual tension that was crackling around them as loudly as the fire in the fireplace. "Meadow—"

"I'm afraid," she whispered, turning the hand that he held so that she could curl her fingers around his, clinging to him.

"I know you are," he said, settling his other hand on her thigh. If he didn't know it was a really bad idea he'd kiss her just to take her fear away, even for a second. He'd even go so far as to throw her down, rip off her clothes, and make love to her until the sun rose if it made her feel better. "But I will protect you from him. I won't let him ever lay a hand on you again. Tell me his name so I can arrest him."

Helplessness shone through those sparkling blue eyes of hers, but she kept her mouth shut. Whatever this man had done to her was enough that she was scared into silence. If Meadow wasn't going to tell him who the man was then he would find out himself, because there was no way he was letting this beautiful, sweet woman fall into that vicious psychopath's hands.

No way.

FEBRUARY 6TH

3:38 A.M.

Screams.

Someone was screaming.

Meadow woke in a panic.

He was here.

In the house.

He'd found her.

She had no idea how he managed to keep tracking her down, not that it mattered now, he was here, and he was going to take her away with him.

Meadow fought, and it wasn't until she landed on the floor on her knees with a loud thud that she realized she had been fighting with her blankets.

There was no one in her room.

He wasn't here.

A dream?

Had the screams just been a dream?

She didn't remember dreaming about him, but that didn't mean that she hadn't. She might have forgotten the dream as soon as she woke up.

Taking long deep breaths, gradually her heart rate began to slow. She was amazed she had been able to fall asleep at all given the accident and the tension that had bubbled between her and Abe while he'd been tending to the cut on her head.

She'd wanted him to kiss her.

If she'd been braver she would have begged him to.

Maybe if she wasn't such a …

Her train of thought was interrupted, and she jerked upright when she heard the scream again. She was definitely awake this time so it wasn't just a dream. It had to be Abe. He must have broken in here once they'd fallen asleep and decided to take out Abe before he came for her.

Her instincts were telling her to run.

To run and never ever even contemplate stopping again.

She had to get out of here before he finished with Abe and came for her.

Meadow was halfway down the stairs when she realized she couldn't do this. She couldn't just run and leave Abe to his mercy. The man she was running from never showed any mercy, and Abe was in this mess because of her, she couldn't not try to help him.

Turning around, she crept back up the stairs, searching for a weapon as she went. She found an umbrella and picked it up, clutching it so tightly her knuckles turned white.

With her pulse drumming in her ears and her entire body shaking like she'd been drenched in ice water, Meadow tiptoed into Abe's bedroom to find …

Nothing.

Abe was lying under a crisp white sheet on his bed, fast asleep.

Maybe she was losing her mind.

Imagining screams when there were none.

It was probably just knowing that he had killed two people today, that he had made an attempt to kidnap her, and the reality of the fact that he was never going to let her be free was messing with her head.

Just as she turned to leave, Abe screamed in the bed behind her.

So she wasn't crazy, it was Abe's screams that had awakened her, he must be having a nightmare.

Should she wake him?

Were you supposed to wake someone who was having a nightmare?

No, it was sleepwalking where you weren't supposed to wake someone, she was pretty sure that it would be okay to wake Abe. She certainly didn't want to hear him scream again. He was so big, so strong, and she needed to believe that he was big enough and strong enough to protect her if *he* came back.

Tentatively, she walked to the bed and reached out a hand, stopping just shy of touching him. "Abe?"

He didn't hear her and began to thrash in his sleep.

"Abe?" she said again, a little louder this time, and she lightly touched her fingertips to his shoulder.

His reaction was instantaneous.

Abe lurched upright, his fist connected with her chest, flinging her backward and into the wall. He snatched up a gun from the nightstand and then he was standing over her, breathing hard, the weapon aimed directly at her head.

"Meadow," he said when he realized it was her. "I'm so sorry."

She tried to answer, but he'd hit her right where the seatbelt had bruised her ribs in the car accident, and she couldn't draw a proper breath.

"Did I hurt you? Are you okay?" he asked, setting the gun down and scooping her into his arms, putting her on the bed. "I'm so sorry, I didn't know it was you, I just felt someone touch me and reacted."

Since he was rambling and Abe never rambled, she drew in as much of a breath as she could and murmured, "It's okay. I'm okay."

"No you're not," he said, his hazel eyes filled with remorse.

"I really am," she assured him as he plumped up pillows and eased her back to rest upon them. "You were having a nightmare, I heard screaming, I thought it was *him*."

"I'm sorry," he said again.

She didn't want his apologies, she didn't need them, he hadn't done anything wrong, she knew all about nightmares. Sometimes the worst kind of nightmares weren't the ones filled with monsters, they were the ones filled with happiness because then you had to wake up and find you really were with a monster. Since Abe was obviously upset about hurting her she tried to change the subject. "What was your dream about?"

His eyes grew dark, and she thought he wasn't going to answer. She couldn't blame him, it wasn't like she had been forthcoming about her past, and she was sure he must have seen some horrendous things while he was in the military.

"It's okay, you don't have to tell me," she said quickly. Her chest no longer felt like it was about to explode, so she may as well get out of here and get back to bed.

When she moved to get off the bed he stopped her. "Stay," he said simply. "The dream was about my ex."

"You were married?" she asked, not sure how much she should pry.

"Engaged. My high school sweetheart. I enlisted as soon as I graduated, and we thought we were in love, I proposed, and she said yes, said she would wait for me."

"She lied?" Meadow asked, reading between the lines.

"Leaving her was hard, but the marines were in my blood, and I knew I wanted to do a tour before I came home to her and we decided what the rest of our lives looked like. She said she was okay with that. I missed her every day I was gone, I called when I could, sent emails when I could, I dreamed about what our lives would be like, but I was happy with what I was doing. It was hard. I lost a lot of friends, had my fair share of close calls, but the closest was a woman who put explosives in a bassinette with her two-month-old son knowing we would go up to the abandoned baby, try to help him, that bomb took out nearly a dozen men."

Even though she knew Abe wasn't one of them her heart clenched as she realized how close he had come to dying. How could a mother do that to her own baby? Absently her hand rested on her stomach, she might have mixed feelings about her own baby, but she couldn't imagine doing anything to hurt it.

"The day I came home to her I felt like I was starting my life over, it was a whole new world, and I was looking forward to sharing it with her. And then that dream was over. I walked into our house and found her in bed with another man."

"Oh, Abe, I'm so sorry." With an unsure hand she reached out and gently rested it on top of his.

"I lost it, I had never been so angry in my life. She started screaming, telling me that when I left, I left her pregnant, and stress caused her to lose the baby. She blamed me. Said it was my fault."

There was so much pain in his words, this big, tough man was just a big softie inside, and she wanted to take away his pain. "That was unfair of her to blame you," she said passionately. "You were risking your life to keep her safe, to make sure that baby had a safe place to grow up. If she didn't see what a wonderful guy she had and threw that away then that was her loss."

Abe quirked one side of his mouth up into a smile. "Thank you."

She felt herself blush at the way he was looking at her. Abe was a hard guy to read, he didn't give much away, and she wasn't even sure if he had felt the same heated desire that had brewed between them last night.

She liked him.

She was attracted to him.

She wanted to get to know him better.

She could see him as someone she could fall in love with.

She could see them having a future.

But what did he see when he looked at her?

* * * * *

4:01 A.M.

She was blushing.

Meadow was so adorable when she blushed.

Her gaze skittered around the room, and Abe wondered what she was thinking. She'd been supportive when he'd told her about the mess his first relationship had disintegrated into, taking his side, and although he wished he hadn't woken her with his screams he wasn't embarrassed about it. He'd seen things while he was in the marines that no person should ever see, and it had left a mark on him that nothing could ever erase. It was a part of him, but that Meadow just accepted that without even saying anything was sweet, and it made him want to kiss her even more than he had last night when he'd ached to take away her fear.

But kissing Meadow would be a mistake.

Because she needed stability right now, she needed a foundation to build her life on. She was pregnant and hiding from a vicious killer. She was about the last woman on the planet he should be thinking about getting involved with because he didn't do stability.

He didn't do relationships either.

What he did do was one night stands.

He was quite the expert at them, but Meadow wasn't the kind of woman you did that with. She was the kind of woman who deserved it all, the whole dating, marriage, kids, dogs, white picket fence, everything.

"I'm running from my husband," Meadow suddenly blurted out.

Okay, he hadn't expected her to admit it.

The first thought he had was that he hated that she was married, even if it was to a violent psychopath.

The second was that she was in so much danger.

The third was that he had to get as much information as he

could out of her so that he could send her husband to prison for the rest of his life.

"Your husband abused you," he said gently, a statement not a question.

Meadow's eyes shimmered with unshed tears, and she nodded slowly.

"Is he a doctor? Is that why you're afraid of them?"

"No. He had a friend, he'd come around sometimes when my husband hurt me too badly but didn't want to take me to the hospital."

"You're husband, he's a killer too, isn't he?"

Meadow shook her head so quickly she sent a couple of tears tumbling down her cheeks. "He's not. He never hurt anyone, only me."

The way she said *only me* had his blood boiling. She said it like she wasn't worth worrying about, like she was nothing, and that he shouldn't really blame this guy for whatever he did to her.

Grabbing her arm with enough force that her eyes widened and she trembled in his hold, he shoved her sleeve up and ran his finger along a white line that ran from the back of her wrist halfway up to her elbow. "He did this to you? What did he use? A knife? A switchblade? A razor? Did he like watching you bleed? Did it turn him on? Did he want you to scream while he cut you? Did he like watching tears trickle down your cheeks just like they are right now?" Abruptly he released her arm and touched the pad of his forefinger to her wet cheek, catching the tears that fell. "So you think you deserved all of that?"

"N-no, well, y-yes," she stammered, uncertainty blooming in her face.

He was the sheriff, he knew how this went. Her husband would have isolated her, drilled into her that she was worthless, while terrifying her into keeping what he did to her quiet because no one was going to believe her anyway. He hated the way these predators preyed on the vulnerable, and growing up feeling lost and alone with no one to love her had made Meadow susceptible to this man's advances.

"I was tired of being alone, I was tired of having no one, all I wanted was someone to love me, but no one even blinked twice in my direction. I wanted to just stand up in a crowd and scream *I'm here* to see if anyone even noticed me. I felt invisible. And then I met him. He made me feel alive. He was the first person who ever said he cared, who ever told me that he loved me. Do you know how stupid I felt when I realized that it was all just a lie? He didn't love me, all he wanted was someone stupid enough to give themselves up to him willingly."

"He manipulated you," he gritted out.

"I went to him willingly," she countered.

"How old were you?"

"Nineteen, but I knew what I was doing, at least I thought I did. Until I moved in with him." Her blue eyes clouded over, and when she spoke it was like she was reciting things she had been told. "I'm not very pretty, I'm not very smart, and I'm weak, it's no wonder nobody ever wanted me. That's why my mother gave me away, that's why I was never adopted as a child, and that's why no one ever wanted to date me, there was nothing in me that made me worthy, nothing that—"

With a growl, Abe grabbed Meadow, dragged her off the bed, and shoved her up against the wall. His mouth descended on hers, kissing her like he'd wanted to ever since he saw her walk into that diner. She tasted sweet, and although she was surprised at first she quickly pressed her body into his, her hands lifted to his hair, and her fingers twirled through it.

This was a bad idea.

Abe knew it was and yet he made no move to stop.

Instead, he curled one hand around her bottom, dragging her closer so she was all but plastered against him. His other hand touched her breast and began to knead, enjoying the way she moaned into his mouth under his ministrations.

Why was he doing this?

Meadow had already been used and taken advantage of by one cold-hearted monster, and now she was being taken advantage of by another. Okay, so maybe he wasn't a monster, but he was definitely cold-hearted, and even on his best day, he didn't deserve someone as sweet and innocent as Meadow.

Finally, he snapped to his senses and gently pushed her away.

"Don't stop," Meadow begged, her eyes heavy with lust and she tried to draw him back down to kiss her again.

"Meadow, we can't," he tried to keep his voice soft, not let any of the mixed-up mess of emotions that were swirling around inside him show.

"Why? Because I'm still married?" she asked.

No. Although that was definitely part of it. He didn't do married women even if that woman had been tricked into marriage by a psychopath who only wanted to hurt her while she was only a teenager.

"Because your husband wants you back, because he somehow followed you here and killed two people."

"No." She shook her head firmly. "He's not a killer. I swear he's not. He's an evil man, and he hurt me badly." Shame filled her face and voice, and he hated that her husband had made her feel like she was unworthy, that she was nothing. "He's not a killer, Abe. I don't know who killed your two victims, but it wasn't him."

"Then who ran you off the road?" he asked. He knew that he was right, Meadow was just in denial because she couldn't cope with the possibility that he might somehow get her back.

"N-no one," she stuttered.

"Then why do you have this cut?" His fingers touched lightly at the edge of the gash on her forehead. Then he let his fingers trail down her cheek, pausing when they reached the hollow of her neck where her pulse was pounding, then he put his hand on her chest. "And who bruised your ribs? Someone ran you off the road, and according to Billy and Darren Sutton, that person hightailed it out of there as soon as they showed up. I know you don't want to face it, but he managed to find you, and now he's killing people and leaving dozens of flowers behind. He's making his own meadow. I need you to tell me his name. I need you to tell me where you came from and everything you can about him so I can find him before he gets what he wants. You."

Meadow's plump pink lips pressed into a narrow line, she was shutting down again. The possibility that her plan to run hadn't worked was too much for her to cope with at the moment, but she didn't have a choice. Her husband *was* coming for her.

The need to stop the man had suddenly taken on a whole new dimension. Meadow was too special to wind up back in the hellhole she had fought so hard to escape.

She needed to realize that everything her husband had told her about herself wasn't true. She wasn't weak, stupid, or ugly. In fact she was the opposite of all those things.

His hand still rested on her chest, and he could feel her heart hammering wildly. "You're a beautiful woman, Meadow, it's not you who has the problem, it's him. You ran away. You're clearly terrified of him, and you're carrying his baby, but you ran because you knew that if you stayed you and your baby were going to be hurt, I wouldn't say that a weak person could do that. You're a strong woman, Meadow. Strong and beautiful."

Because he needed one last kiss, he curled a hand around the back of her neck and dipped his head, whispering his lips across hers before he turned and walked out of the room.

* * * * *

12:48 P.M.

He could still feel Meadow's lips on his own.

Still smell the lavender shampoo she used, still taste her sweet mouth, still feel her soft body pressed up against his.

Abe knew he was in big trouble.

He felt like such a jerk. He was leading her on, letting her think that maybe there could be something between them, that they had a future, that a relationship might be in the cards, and that wasn't true.

There would never be anything between them.

Well, maybe friendship—but if he was completely honest probably not that either—but there wouldn't ever be anything more. He wasn't in the market for a girlfriend, he'd done the whole getting engaged thing already, and all he'd gotten out of it was a dead baby and a boatload of guilt.

He wasn't going through that again.

But Meadow was vulnerable right now, she was seeking stability and a fresh start, she wanted a life where she and her baby could be free, where they could live their lives without fear, and he didn't want her to think that his home was going to be that place.

"You haven't been listening to a word I said," Julian said.

Abe blinked to clear his vision and realized that what his cousin had said was true. He was at work, he was dealing with two murders in his quiet little paradise, plus Meadow being run off the road. He really needed to focus.

And yet he couldn't.

Every time he tried, his thoughts invariably returned to Meadow and that kiss.

He was in trouble.

Really big trouble.

The more he kept telling himself that he wasn't interested in a relationship and that he was only helping Meadow because it was the right thing to do, the less he believed it.

"What is going on with you today?" Julian asked. "We have two dead people. Two *murdered* dead people. You're the sheriff, it's kinda your job to figure out who did it and why."

"I know who did it."

"Oh?" Julian raised a brow. "You know who the killer is?"

"I don't know his name, but it's Meadow's husband." Abe hated that word, especially in conjunction with Meadow. Why did she have to be married? Why did it even matter that she was married? It wasn't like he intended to do anything about his attraction to her so it didn't matter that she was already married. All that mattered was finding her husband before he came for her because even though he wasn't interested in her, he didn't want to see anything bad happen to her.

"Meadow is married?"

"Apparently." Part of his brain—the part that seemed to be fueled by hormones and not common sense—wished that she was unattached. Although he should be happy that she wasn't available, the fact that she was married should make it easier to keep his hands off her. Pity his mind didn't work like that. If he wanted her he'd take her, the fact that she had a husband wouldn't get in the way of that. The man was a piece of filth who had tricked a vulnerable teenager into marriage. That marriage was nothing more than a piece of paper.

"She told you that the killer was her husband?" Julian asked.

"Not exactly. She told me that the man she was running from was her husband, but she claims he wouldn't hurt anyone but her and that he's not the one who ran her off the road, but I don't buy it."

"Does she know how he followed her here? This isn't really the kind of place you'd just stumble upon if you're looking for your punching bag," Julian pointed out.

"So you think it's just a coincidence that Meadow is on the run and someone ran her car off the road and then drove off when someone else showed up?" In his mind—in his *gut*—he knew that Meadow's husband, the hit and run, and the murders were all connected. They were all perpetrated by the same man.

"Maybe Meadow getting run off the road was an accident, a

drunk tourist perhaps, he goes to check that the other person is okay, but he panics when someone else shows up worrying that he'll get in trouble."

"I suppose," Abe huffed. It was a plausible theory and although it made sense his gut was telling him that wasn't what had happened. "And maybe I could believe that, but someone murdered Aaron Turner for the sole purpose of stealing his car, then they murdered Carla Briscoe and left her in that car surrounded by a meadow's worth of flowers."

"Murdered doesn't really quantify what he did to Carla," Julian muttered.

He couldn't argue with that.

Murdered didn't even begin to describe what that man had done to Carla Briscoe. The nineteen-year-old had been beaten, caned, raped, and sodomized before he killed her.

"The medical examiner said she was still alive when he put the knife in her," Julian said, his face hard, but he could see the slight quiver in the corner of his cousin's mouth, and Abe knew how affected he was by Carla's murder.

Julian wasn't the only one.

What that man—Meadow's husband—had done to Carla was perhaps one of the most vicious things he had seen one human being do to another. While he had seen a lot in his years in the marines, life in River's End had been quiet. There wasn't a lot of crime here and that was the way he liked it, and now since Meadow's arrival there had been two murders, it was all connected to her. Her husband had somehow found where she was, and he was determined to make her suffer before he took her back.

"It's Meadow's husband, Julian," he said quietly. He didn't want to spend time convincing his deputies that these cases were related to his houseguest, he just wanted to find out who the man was and get him behind bars before anyone else died.

His cousin sighed but nodded. "Okay, let's say you're right—

and I'm not saying that you're not, just trying to remain a little more objective than some other people." He arched a pointed brow. "So if it is her husband, how are you going to get her to start talking? He tortured and slaughtered that poor woman, and stabbed that nice Mr. Turner over a dozen times just for his car."

Mr. Turner was an elderly man, nearing ninety, who was still very active for his age, he went fishing and hunting, and he baked the most amazing gingerbread boys and girls for all the children in the town every Christmas. Although he was quiet and kept mostly to himself, the man was sweet, and everyone in the town loved him. That he had fallen victim to this killer was a tragedy and was most likely a crime of opportunity. Mr. Turner lived alone about two miles outside of the town and fit as he was for a ninety-year-old man, he would still have made an easy mark.

Who was going to be next?

There was no way the killer was just going to move on. If he was here for Meadow, he would keep killing as he circled closer waiting for his opportunity to grab her.

"Did CSU find anything on either victim or the car?" he asked. Since he'd rushed off yesterday afternoon as soon as he heard about Meadow being run off the road, he hadn't been there when they arrived.

"According to their report, they didn't find anything. Looks like he was careful with each of the murders, and he wiped down the car with bleach before he put the flowers in it and left," Julian replied.

"So we have nothing," he growled, frustrated. Meadow was his responsibility as long as she was staying in his home and he wasn't going to lose her on his watch. He hadn't been there for Talia when she was pregnant, and whether the stress of being alone had been what caused the miscarriage or not he hadn't been there for his baby either. There was no way he was going to lose another baby, and if Meadow's unborn child got in the hands of her husband he was sure the child would be tortured and no doubt molded to be what its father wanted.

"Well, not nothing exactly."

"What do we have then?"

"Meadow. You think that this is her husband then you need to convince her to tell you everything she knows about him. A name might not help us find him, but it will help, and if we know more about him we might be able to figure out his next move. She trusts you, Abe, you have to get her to talk before anyone else in our town dies."

Making Meadow talk to keep his town safe made him feel like he was using her, but this was about keeping her safe too, so like it or not, he was going to have to find a way to get her talking.

He wondered whether kissing her would work.

* * * * *

6:23 P.M.

She hoped Abe would be home soon.

She knew that he had a job with unpredictable hours, and he had two murders that he was working on solving, so she didn't really know what time to expect him, but she hoped it was soon because otherwise dinner would be ruined.

At work today, she had tried to surreptitiously get out of Maggie what Abe's favorite meal was and was cooking it for him for dinner. Right now the steak was sizzling, the biscuits and gravy were just about ready, and the cornbread was in the oven. She'd started a fire in the fireplace, and she had all the ingredients ready to make S'mores later.

It was all going to be perfect.

After Abe kissed her this morning she had thought about running. She couldn't get involved with another man, she was still married and wasn't sure that it was a good idea even if she wasn't. She had a baby on the way, and she had to build a life for the two of them, even thinking about another man was a stupid idea.

A really stupid idea.

Meadow knew that, and yet as soon as she had nixed the idea of running and trying to start over someplace else all she had been able to think about was that kiss. As ridiculous as it was, she was developing feelings for him. Abe was everything that she had ever wanted in a man, he was strong, confident, sweet on the inside even though he tried to hide it, and treated her respectfully. He was exactly what she had thought her husband was when he was luring her into his trap.

Only Abe would never do that.

He was a good man, and she knew he would be a good husband and a good father to her baby. It would all be so perfect, they could live here in his adorable little cabin, the baby could have the room she was sleeping in now since she'd be sharing Abe's room and his bed. In the summer they'd take the baby swimming in the river, they'd have so much fun, splashing and laughing. In the winter they'd make snowmen, in the fall they'd rake the leaves into big piles and jump in them, and in the spring they'd plant millions of flowers. She would cook dinner for them every night, and then they'd sit together in the living room and watch TV or play games, and then they'd tuck the baby into bed and read it stories before singing it to sleep.

Everything would be the way it should be.

Tonight was going to be the first step in making that happen. While she and Abe were eating dinner, she was going to tell him that she was falling for him. She was expecting him to tell her that it was too soon to even be thinking about developing feelings for one another, but she would easily counter that with the fact that *he* had kissed *her*. Why would he do that if he wasn't feeling the same things that she was?

Was that his car?

Meadow ran to the window and looked out, and just as she'd thought, headlights lit up the night, and he parked his car in the driveway.

This was it, she hoped that things worked out well. She really did like Abe, it wasn't just about needing someone to take care of her, and she really could see them falling in love and having an amazing life together, but he was going to be a tough nut to crack. He was always so composed, he kept his feelings tightly bottled away, and she was sure he would be resistant to the idea of them being a couple. At least at first.

"Abe." She beamed at him as he came through the door. "You're home."

"What smells amazing?" he asked.

"I'm cooking you dinner; steak, cornbread, biscuits and gravy, and S'mores for dessert," she said, hurrying to the stove to take the steak off, then buzzing about dishing up the food.

"My favorites," he said as he came over to the kitchen.

"Well, I might have talked to Maggie and found out what you like so I could cook you dinner. Kind of like a thank you dinner, you know, for everything you've done for me. Letting me stay here in your home, and getting me a job. I know it's not enough, but I just wanted to do something nice for you." Tentatively, she lifted her hand and placed it on his. She wasn't good at the whole dating thing, her husband had been much older than her and had been the dominant one in the relationship even before he let his abusive streak show.

"Meadow," he started, and the tone of his voice said she wasn't going to like what he was about to say.

"Dinner's ready," she cut him off. She didn't want him to put a dampener on this night. In her head she had pictured them eating, talking about each other, laughing and enjoying the evening, and then they would do a little more kissing before they went up to bed. Separate beds of course, she wasn't ready to sleep with him. Not only did she not sleep with guys she'd just met, but she'd also only ever been with two men, and one of them didn't make love to her, he basically threw her on the bed and did what he wanted to her regardless of how she felt about it or what she wanted.

"Meadow, stop," he said, taking hold of her shoulders when she turned to finish dishing up dinner and turning her around to face him. "I know what you're trying to do and it's my fault. It's the kiss, I shouldn't have done that."

She gasped.

He regretted the kiss?

She thought he had kissed her because he wanted her so why was he backtracking?

"It was a mistake, Meadow, I shouldn't have done it, I'm sorry." His hazel eyes bored into hers, beseeching her to believe him.

A mistake.

While she had spent the day reliving the kiss and daydreaming about what their future might be like, he had spent the day regretting it ever happened.

Mortified tears burned the backs of her eyes, but she fought them. She was so tired of always being the victim. "Of course you think it was a mistake. You just see me as some poor, pathetic girl who needs someone to look after her, and you know what? You're right, I am."

"No, you're not," he said firmly, but she didn't believe him.

How stupid could she be?

Of course he didn't want to have a future with her. Fantasizing about what their lives could have been like was so ridiculous. Why did she always have to do this? Why was she always so desperate to be loved that she didn't see things for what they were?

"You don't believe that," she accused.

"I do. Meadow, I think the fact that you ran from this man proves how strong you are. You're not pathetic, and you are fully capable of looking after yourself."

"Then why do you think the kiss was a mistake?" she demanded, wishing she didn't sound so needy.

"Because you're already thinking about the two of us as a

couple and I don't want a relationship," he said.

She could tell he was trying to be gentle with her, his tone was soft, and his eyes were pleading, and the hands that still rested on her shoulders were massaging. But she didn't want gentle. She wanted him to like her because she liked him, and although it sounded so childish it was exactly how she felt.

"Then why did you kiss me?"

"Because I think you're beautiful, but we want two different things out of life. I'm sorry, I shouldn't have done it, and if I'd known that you were reading more into it I would have been clearer this morning about what the kiss meant to me."

"Nothing. It meant nothing to you," she said dully. She really was an idiot. He didn't feel anything for her, she was just his charity case, he was doing his good deed for the year.

That was it.

Nothing more.

She had to stop picturing a perfect future with someone who would love her. That was never going to happen for her, it was time to accept it. The only one who would love her forever was the baby growing inside her. From here on out it was just the two of them.

Extricating herself from Abe's grip, she silently turned around and walked out of the kitchen, heading upstairs to her room. She'd take a shower—it might be the last one she could take for a while—then she'd put on the clothes she was wearing when she ran from her husband, take a nap, and then as soon as Abe went to sleep she was leaving.

* * * * *

7:04 P.M.

So much for trying to protect Meadow.

This was not how he envisioned the evening turning out. He'd planned on sitting her down and gently broaching the topic of the kiss, telling her that it shouldn't have happened, then trying to get her to open up about her husband so he could find the man and throw him behind bars.

Instead, he'd come home to find her cooking his favorite meal, a smile lighting her face when she saw him, excitement vibrating off her. It was obvious she had a whole fantasy in her head about how the night was going to pan out, and he hadn't had any choice but to be blunt with her. In doing so he'd hurt her again, and while he hated shattering her hopes and dreams, it was better than misleading her and letting her believe that something was going to happen between them.

He was doing the right thing, so why did he feel so awful?

With a sigh, Abe took the last of the food off the stove and took a plate and sat down with it at the table. How had she managed to find out what his favorite dinner was?

It was sweet.

She was sweet.

He'd never dated a sweetheart before. Things with his fiancée had been hot and heavy, but she definitely hadn't been sweet, she was one of those sexy girls who knew she was beautiful and used it to get her way. But Meadow had no idea that she was pretty, and somehow that made her even more attractive.

If she wasn't who she was, and she hadn't been through what she had, then he probably would have had a couple of nights of amazing sex, then when he had her husband locked up where he belonged he would have sent her on her way confident that they had both gotten what they wanted. But Meadow wasn't that kind of woman. She had been mistreated and abused and was just trying to find her way in the world, she needed support not sex while she did that.

Poking at the food on his plate, he realized he couldn't eat this. Meadow had made it with the intention of the two of them bonding. To eat it alone while she was upstairs no doubt crying, seemed wrong.

Leaving the food on the table, he grabbed a mac and cheese packet from the cupboard and filled up a pot with water. The meal wasn't anywhere near as good as what Meadow had made, but it would suffice. In the morning, he'd try to talk to Meadow again, explain things better, but tonight he'd just give her some space.

Abe stood and watched as the water started to boil. The little bubbles popped and more took their place, it was almost mesmerizing, the bubbles grew bigger, and the sloshing sound seemed to penetrate his brain until the whole world was nothing more than the bubbling water.

When his phone rang, he practically jumped a mile.

Turning the stove off, he pulled out his cell. "Hey, Julian."

"I've got news that's going to make you happy."

"Oh yeah?" News that was going to make him happy was exactly what he needed right now.

"We found the car that ran Meadow off the road," his cousin told him.

Billy and Darren Sutton had arrived on the scene just moments after Meadow had hit that tree, effectually saving her life, so they had the license plate of the car, they just hadn't been able to find it. "Had it been set alight?"

"Nope," Julian replied, and he could practically hear the smile in his deputy's voice.

Since the day wasn't going well, he hadn't been expecting the news to be all that good and any criminal worth his salt would have torched the car as soon as he was away from the scene so there would be no evidence left behind, apparently he'd been wrong though. "Have CSU gone through it yet?"

"They're on the scene right now, but there's blood in the vehicle."

Blood in the vehicle. If they could connect the blood to Aaron Turner or Carla Briscoe then maybe that would get Meadow talking. "Keep me updated, I want to know the second you have anything."

"How's it going with Meadow?"

"It's not." And after the disaster tonight had turned into, he wasn't liking his chances of making any sort of headway with her ever.

"What's going on? You sound strained, is there a problem?"

"You could say that."

"What happened?"

"I kissed her."

"What?" Julian exclaimed. "You kissed her? You were supposed to be trying to get her to talk not playing tonsil hockey."

"Tonsil hockey?"

"You get my drift. So why did you kiss her?"

"It wasn't tonight, I kissed her this morning."

"And I spent all day with you and you didn't mention it, why?" Julian demanded. His cousin could be such a gossip sometimes.

"Because it was a mistake and I should never have done it."

"You didn't tell Meadow it was a mistake, did you?" When his silence drifted on for close to thirty seconds, he heard Julian sigh. "Why would you tell her that?"

"Because I came home and she had cooked me dinner—my favorite dinner—and it felt like leading her on."

"She cooked you your favorite dinner after you kissed her. Why exactly do you think this is a mistake? Crazy husband aside, Meadow sounds like a really sweet woman. Why aren't you giving this a chance?"

"Do I really need to answer that?" Meadow was everything Julian had said and more, and any man would be lucky to have her, but the bottom line was he didn't do relationships and that hadn't changed.

"Talia was the problem, Abe, not you. Why are you letting something that happened a decade ago ruin what could be the best thing that ever happened to you?"

Why?

Well, he didn't exactly have a good answer for that particular question.

He'd never been that warm and fuzzy guy that wanted to discuss feelings and who was good at communication, and after Talia he'd just gotten more closed off. Meadow had a traumatic marriage to deal with plus a baby on the way, and he was hardly the kind of guy to help her with that.

"Come on, Abe, she's totally into you. Why don't you just roll with it, see where things go?"

"Maybe because her psychotically violent husband is killing people and trying to get her back. Right now, it's not important that Meadow likes me, what *is* important is keeping her alive, so I made a decision."

"What is it?" Julian asked dubiously.

"I don't think Meadow should stay with me anymore. I'd ask Maggie if she can have a room at the hotel since she's working there anyway, but I want her somewhere safe if her husband tries anything else, so I was wondering ..."

"If she could stay with me?" Julian finished his sentence.

"Are you up for it? I know that she's my responsibility, I'm the one who found her, but I just don't think having her here is working out."

"It's fine, it's no big deal. If she's up for it, she can stay with me until we get this sorted out. That is if she agrees."

Julian was right. Meadow was uncomfortable around strangers, and there was a chance that she was going to run if he told her that she'd be moving in with his cousin. But it was a chance he was willing to take because he couldn't keep a clear head around her, and that meant he was distracted which might lead to Meadow getting hurt and that he couldn't allow that to happen.

"I'll convince her it's the best thing for everyone," he assured Julian. "Thanks."

"You're welcome. I'll call you if CSU finds anything. And, Abe, think about the whole Meadow thing."

"Sure," he agreed, although he had no intention of spending time thinking about the possibility of him and Meadow as a couple. The less he thought about that the better. Because if he thought about it too much, he just might try to convince himself that they actually might make a good couple. "Night, Julian."

Once he hung up the phone, he finished making his macaroni and cheese, and ate it alone in the kitchen, very aware of the fact that Meadow was just upstairs. When he'd washed the dishes and tidied up, he turned off the lights and went into the living room. He wasn't sure that she wouldn't try to make a run for it, and he wanted to be there to stop her if she tried.

Maybe that was why he was so adamant that he and Meadow weren't meant to be. He'd loved Talia, and not only had she left him but she'd cheated on him and blamed him for her miscarriage. Meadow was still unsure about her decision to stay in River's End. Whenever she felt threatened, self-preservation was going to have her wanting to flee, and if he ever decided that he wanted to give a relationship a second try it wasn't going to be with someone who would run whenever she got scared.

Settling into his comfortable armchair, he prepared himself for a long night.

FEBRUARY 7TH

2:27 A.M.

Meadow stretched out her foot and very carefully placed it on the top step. Her whole body was tense. One wrong move and he would know that she was leaving, and she knew Abe well enough to know that if he found out that she was splitting, he would stop her.

She didn't know why he was bothering.

Abe had made it pretty clear that he wasn't interested in her, so why did he care if she ran? Surely it shouldn't make any difference if she was here or anywhere else in the world, and if her husband really had managed to find her here, she was starting to think that she was never going to be safe no matter where in the world she was.

He was never going to let her go.

He was never going to let her have a life that didn't include him.

He was going to hunt her down until he got his claws back into her and dragged her back with him to that house.

She hated that house.

It had been her prison for so many years. She knew every inch of it, she had traipsed around it so many times, desperate for a way to escape but knowing that there wasn't one.

Now she was free, and it felt so good to have her whole life before her, to be able to make her own choices and go after what she wanted, but he would never let her do it. She should have known that, she should have known that there was no corner of the world where she could hide. It didn't matter how small River's End was he had found her here.

So she had to leave.

That was her only option, and it wasn't like anything was holding her here. She liked Maggie, and she liked working in her restaurant, but that was it. Abe didn't reciprocate the feelings that she had for him so she had no ties here, she could always find another chef job someplace else.

Oh, who was she kidding?

She was never going to settle down someplace.

Meadow had no idea how her husband had found her here, but it proved that no matter where she went he would find her, which meant that she would never be settling down anywhere and getting a job. She would have to keep running, and if she was lucky enough, she would be able to keep one step ahead of him long enough to stay alive.

She wouldn't be able to keep her baby though.

There were no guarantees that she could stay ahead of him and there was no way she was going to let this tiny little baby fall into the hands of someone so evil. The only way she could keep it safe was to let it go, to leave it somewhere anonymously, somewhere that her husband would never find.

Quietly, she moved her second foot down to join her first on the top stair and was thankful it didn't make a sound, and Abe didn't suddenly appear before her, so she proceeded down the staircase with excruciating slowness. Her stomach growled, and she wished that she had time to grab something to eat, but the longer she stayed here, the greater the chances that Abe would find her, so she would have to just leave. With no job and no likelihood of getting one in the near future, she would have to get used to being hungry.

Maybe if she was lucky, hunger or the elements would claim her before her husband could get to her. She'd be dead either way, but at least she'd save herself a whole lot of suffering.

He was going to be so angry with her.

She'd spent years trying her best to deflect his anger by doing anything and everything she could to make him happy, but there would be no escaping this punishment. Meadow wondered whether she would survive it. She had defied him in the worst possible way, not only had she left, but she'd taken his child along with her, and she was pretty sure that the punishment for that would be death.

Her own and maybe the baby's too.

She knew he didn't care about the child, it was just a possession to him, and she truly wouldn't be surprised if he ripped it from her womb and killed it in front of her just to show her that he could and that he was the boss of her.

Meadow reached the bottom of the stairs, Abe hadn't shown up so he was obviously asleep meaning she could slip away quietly, and by the time he woke up in the morning and realized she wasn't there, she would be long gone. Since she had no money for a bus ticket this time she would have to risk hitchhiking. It could land her with another psychopath, but what other choice did she have?

She could always take some money from Abe before she left.

No.

She couldn't steal from him, not after everything he had done for her.

When she'd left it had taken her months to scrounge enough spare change and keep a little extra from the money he gave her to do the grocery shopping. Stealing from her husband was different, although in most marriages everything was considered to be shared, that wasn't the case with her marriage. Everything, including her, belonged to him. He would have punished her if he had found out what she was doing, but he was abusing her and she needed out, so she hadn't had a choice, she'd had to take the money so she could flee.

But she would never do that to Abe.

So hitchhiking it was.

She tiptoed the short distance from the bottom of the staircase to the front door, and without looking back, she eased the door open and slipped out into the cold night.

That first gust of icy wind seemed to slice straight through her and she very nearly retreated back inside the house, but she couldn't. She had to get out of there. She had to do whatever it took to keep herself alive, and right now, that meant running.

Meadow was so preoccupied with the fact that Abe might come bursting out of his cabin at any moment that she didn't notice the truck until the headlights lit up the night.

She gasped.

It was him.

Without pausing, Meadow turned and ran.

She didn't get far.

"Well, my pet, you thought you could run from me?" the voice of her nightmares growled in her ear as a strong hand clamped around her shoulder, yanking her backward and holding her against a chest as hard as a rock.

She hadn't made it.

It was over.

"You can't even imagine how bad your punishment is going to be," he said as he dragged her toward his truck. Once he got her inside it really would be over. He would take her away, and no one would ever find her. She would be his prisoner until he decided to kill her.

Meadow struggled in his grip but it was like a vice, there was no getting out of it. She could scream, Abe would hear it and come running, but she was terrified that that would only get him killed. He might not feel anything for her, but she had feelings for him, and she wouldn't risk him getting hurt.

Which left her with no choices.

"Miss me, sweetheart?" he asked when they got to the car.

Experience had taught her never to answer any question he asked her unless he expressly said he wanted to hear her talk.

So she stayed silent and tried not to look at him.

He was so angry, she could feel it vibrating off him, and she wondered if he would even get her back to the house before he killed her. She'd never seen him like this before. His dark eyes glittered like two black holes in the night, his hair was wild, framing his head in a dark mess of wild curls. He was evil personified and she didn't know how she had ever fallen for his act.

"You are going to pray for death before I'm done with you," he hissed as he curled one hand around her neck, squeezing hard enough so that she could just suck in enough air to remain conscious, but still make her panic about her airways being closed. His other hand roughly shoved its way into the waistband of her jeans, and he pushed a finger inside her. "You're my wife, you think you can just leave me, you think you can take this away from me?" he asked, stroking harshly inside her as her body flinched and tried to pull away from him.

But like always there was no place to go.

She had put herself in this situation, she had no one to blame but herself.

She had given herself to him, and she had gotten pregnant by him, and she had run away only to wind up back with him.

The world started to gray around the edges, the pressure on her throat slowly choking the life out of her as his finger inside her tore away another piece of her soul.

* * * * *

2:59 A.M.

The small bassinette stood out.

Bright white against the brown, dusty landscape.

Something was wrong.

Abe knew that.

No one would leave a baby alone out in the hot sun.

Still, he walked toward it.

It was like his feet couldn't stop even if they wanted to.

When he reached the bassinette, he lifted the blanket.

A baby that looked just like him stared up at him, tears falling down its little cheeks.

Then he saw it.

The bomb.

It was counting down the seconds in bright red digits.

Red.

The color of blood.

Abe went to pick up the baby, but when he tried, he found a chain with a padlock attached to the baby's ankle.

Keys.

A whole ring full of them.

He had no choice, one by one he had to try them in the lock.

The timer ticked down, mocking him.

The baby cried.

The clock ticked.

Key after key didn't fit.

Then the bomb exploded.

White light blanketed them.

Abe blinked and opened his eyes, surprised to find that even though he was awake now, he was still bathed in light.

It took only a split second for his instincts to kick in.

Headlights.

Someone was out there.

He snatched up his phone, but there were no missed calls or messages so he knew it wasn't one of his brothers or cousins, they would know better than to turn up unannounced, especially when he had Meadow here, and her husband was on the loose.

Which meant it had to be Meadow's husband.

No one else would be here in the middle of the night, and since the vehicle had its headlights on, Meadow must be out there. She'd been going to run, and she must have stumbled upon him, and if he didn't hurry up and do something they'd be gone and he'd never see her again.

He couldn't allow that to happen.

Grabbing his gun, he moved to the window, easing back the drapes so he could see out. The headlights blinded him, and they blackened everything around them making it hard for him to get his bearings. While Abe hated going into a situation blind, it didn't look like he had a choice. He had to do something, and Meadow's husband wasn't stupid, he wasn't going to hang around long, especially now that he had what he wanted.

Quietly, he walked through the house and drew in a deep breath, he was only going to have one shot at this and it had to work.

Throwing open the door, he aimed his gun at the headlights. "It's the sheriff, you need to step away from the vehicle." Now that he was out there he could see that the driver's door of the truck was open, and a huge man was standing there, towering over Meadow. The man had his hands around her neck.

No, not hands.

One hand was around her neck; the other was down her pants.

"She's not yours, Sheriff, so don't interfere, unless you want me to kill more people here in your charming little town," the man threatened.

He wasn't playing that game. He wasn't going to sacrifice Meadow to keep the people in River's End safe, he could do both.

"Last chance," Abe said, giving a warning of his own.

The man wasn't going to listen, he already had Meadow, all he had to do was drag her with him into the car and they'd be out of here. Already he could see that the shadowy figure had removed his hand from her jeans and was pulling her backward.

Since he couldn't risk hitting Meadow, Abe aimed at the

ground, right at their feet, and fired off a shot.

The man swore but he also released Meadow.

"Meadow, run," he yelled. He didn't have time to get to her, he needed to get this man in cuffs.

Meadow took off into the woods at his order, and her husband launched himself sideways and into the truck. Abe fired off another shot, this time aiming for the tires, but the other man was obviously armed as well because a bullet suddenly rammed into the wall beside him and wood chips flew around him.

He had no choice but to retreat into the house, which gave Meadow's husband enough time to take off up his driveway.

Abe had to make a choice, get in his car and try to follow the man, or go and find Meadow, who was alone and unprotected, running through the woods, no doubt terrified out of her mind.

It wasn't a hard choice to make.

Shoving his gun into his waistband, he grabbed his jacket, and thankful that he had never gotten around to taking off his boots when he settled into the armchair in his living room, Abe took off in the direction Meadow had gone.

There was a chance that her husband had only driven a short distance away before stopping and going in search of Meadow, so Abe kept his wits about him as he ran, keeping his eyes and ears peeled for any sounds or movements that would indicate that he wasn't alone. Meadow hadn't gotten a huge head start, and she was pregnant as well as scared. He was sure he could catch her, but the forest was thick, and it was almost pitch black out, and just because he knew where she had started didn't mean he knew where she was now.

Gasping.

Abe froze when he could hear someone gasping.

It couldn't be Meadow's husband because there was no way he would allow himself to make a sound, which meant it had to be Meadow.

Getting his bearings, he determined the sounds were coming

from the east and started off that way, moving slower this time, more cautiously.

He hadn't gone more than ten yards or so when he caught sight of her. She was just up ahead and she was staggering along, clutching tree trunk after tree trunk as she went.

She didn't hear him approaching, and it wasn't until he reached out to grab her that she realized he was there.

"No," she shrieked, swinging her small fists at him. She was much smaller than him and he easily batted her hands away, spinning her around and yanking her up against his chest, pinning her arms at her sides and clamping a hand over her mouth.

"Shh," he hushed, "it's just me, Abe, but I need you to be quiet. If he's still out here I don't want you alerting him to where we are. Are you hearing me?"

She was shuddering in his arms, her whole body shaking, and he knew she was crying because her tears were splashing down onto his hand.

"Meadow," he said, deliberately gentling his voice because he knew she was teetering on the edge and might lose it at any moment. "It's okay, I'm here now, we're going to go back to my place, okay?"

She nodded, and tentatively he moved his hand. "Abe," she said it on a sob, and then she was spinning around in his arms and burying her face against his chest as she wept.

Awkwardly, he rubbed her back. He wasn't good with crying women, particularly when he was the reason for the crying. If he hadn't been so blunt with Meadow last night, she wouldn't have been trying to sneak away at two in the morning. If she had been safely tucked up in bed then her husband would never have gotten his filthy hands on her.

Dipping his head, he rested his cheek on the top of Meadow's head, breathing in her scent and attempting to convince himself that she was okay.

"I'm sorry," he whispered, touching his lips to her forehead.

She didn't say anything and he couldn't blame her.

Meadow was shaking, her teeth chattering, and he had to get her back to his cabin, they were too unprotected out here. Her husband could be lurking around anywhere, watching them, waiting to make his move. At the cabin he could protect them. He'd call in his deputies, let them know what happened, and then he'd make arrangements to move Meadow someplace safe.

Shrugging out of his coat, he wrapped it around her shoulders, then scooped her up into his arms and started walking.

"You don't have to carry me," she said softly, and even though it was dark Abe could feel her eyes on him.

He'd made a mess out of things. Meadow was sweet, kind, and thoughtful, and for some reason she seemed to like him, right now, cradling her in his arms, her body warm and soft against him, he couldn't recall why he'd thought that was such a bad thing.

It didn't matter now.

Abe was sure that anything that could have been between them was over now. Meadow had intended to run again, she'd wanted out and he was sure she wasn't going to be pleased when he told her he wanted to lock her away somewhere safe until her husband was caught.

There was no way he was letting her go.

She was his now, he just had to find a way to fix things.

* * * * *

3:13 A.M.

It was hard to breathe.

Meadow could still feel her husband's hand wrapped tightly around her neck even though he was gone now.

She couldn't stop shaking, and her teeth were chattering, both of which were adding to her breathing difficulties.

Abe was carrying her in his arms, she presumed back to his house, and while she should feel safe, she didn't. Her husband had found her, she could no longer pretend that he hadn't, and he had made his intentions clear; she was his and he would reclaim her. She had no say in the matter just like she hadn't had any say in anything else in their marriage.

The urge to curl into Abe, nestle her face against his neck, breathe in his strength and let him take care of her was strong, but she couldn't give in to it. He had made his position clear, he had no feelings for her, and he wasn't going to be developing any anytime soon so she had to accept that.

She was on her own in this.

Which shouldn't surprise her, she had been on her own most of her life. Even while she had lived with her husband she had really been on her own, she'd just been his favorite toy, one he pulled out when he wanted to play, but if he didn't want to play then he expected her to make herself scarce. She was used to being on her own and alone, she had survived everything else life had thrown at her so she could make it through this too.

Meadow wasn't going back with her husband. She would run, she would fight if a chance presented itself, but in the end, she would rather be dead than his prisoner so if it came down to it, she would end her own life before she would let her husband have her back.

Light suddenly washed over them, and a moment later, Abe was carrying her inside his cabin. He paused to close and lock the door behind them, then took her into the living room, set her on the armchair right in front of the fire, which he turned and stoked, making the flames spring to life.

Then he stood and stared at her for a moment.

She didn't want to meet his gaze, she didn't want to see the frustration that must be on his face. Abe had to be tired of her drama. She'd crashed his car, she'd nearly gotten him shot, and he probably wished she had run away so he could be done with her.

His eyes watched her for what felt like forever before he finally sighed and disappeared from the room.

Meadow relaxed, glad she was no longer under scrutiny and concentrated on trying to get more air into her lungs. Her throat was starting to hurt, and she knew he had held it tight enough to leave bruises. Tears were building up but she blinked them back, she had already allowed herself one moment of weakness, one moment to lean against Abe and cry and pretend that she wasn't all alone in the world.

But that was over.

She would have to learn how to toughen up because she had a long and bumpy road ahead of her.

Something heavy was draped over her shoulders, and then Abe was kneeling before her. His hands were big, but when they reached out and lifted her hand, touching his fingers to her wrist to check her pulse, his touch was soft and gentle and her heart fluttered a little.

So much for focusing on being on her own.

Why couldn't a great guy like this ever fall for her?

She'd always been the quiet girl in school, she had friends, and she'd dated a little, but usually the boys gravitated to the bubblier more vivacious girls, not the shy girl with the mousy blonde hair and the tiny breasts and the too skinny figure. She'd been surprised when her husband showed an interest in her, and craving love and affection the way she did, she'd immediately jumped into the relationship.

All she wanted was someone like Abe, good, and kind, and strong, to spend her life with, so why did it never work out that way?

"You're still breathing harshly and I see bruises forming, I know you're in pain, but do you need to go to the hospital?" Abe asked. He'd released her wrist, setting it in her lap, and grasped her chin between his thumb and forefinger, his grip was firm but still gentle.

"I don't need to go to the hospital," she said. Her throat did hurt, and drawing in a breath was a little difficult, but she thought that was probably more because of shock. In her mind nothing had changed, her plans were the same. In fact now more than ever she had to get out of River's End, and being in a hospital would make that more difficult.

Abe's hazel eyes didn't look convinced, but he gave a single, sharp nod. "Are you hurt anywhere else? I know he sexually assaulted you, but I don't know how long you were out there with him. Did he do anything else to you?"

Meadow had gone numb at his words. How many times had her husband sexually assaulted her in their marriage? More than she cared to think about, they'd been together five years, and he enjoyed her pain, sexual or physical or psychological, it didn't matter to him, as long as she was suffering he was happy.

She swallowed audibly, winced as it bothered her throat, then shook her head.

She couldn't manage words at this moment.

"I need his name, Meadow," Abe said. "I know you're scared of him, and I understand why. He's hurt you badly, and I'm sure you have a lot of scars, physical ones and psychological ones, but he's killed two people, and he's made it clear he's going to keep killing people until he gets you. I can't stop him if I don't know who it is I'm looking for."

Right.

He was worried about his town.

She got it, he was the sheriff, it was his job to protect the people of River's End, but she couldn't deny it hurt knowing that whatever affection he had felt for her was gone now.

"Meadow, please," he insisted. "Tell me your husband's name."

What did she have to lose by telling him?

She was leaving here as soon as she got a chance, but maybe having the cops looking for him would give her an advantage as she ran for her life. If she didn't tell him, he could probably eventually find out anyway. She was sure it would take him a while to find the marriage license, her husband knew his way around the law, and she was sure he had made sure that particular license had somehow disappeared, but Abe was a cop, and she knew he would be like a dog with a bone, he would eventually find it.

"His name is John Smith," she whispered, knowing how that sounded.

"John Smith?" Abe arched a brow. "Are you lying to me?"

"No, I swear, that's his name." She met his gaze squarely so he would know that she was telling the truth.

"Okay." He nodded, apparently convinced. "Thank you. We'll put out an APB on him, I don't think he's going to go far, not while you're here. We'll find him, Meadow, and until we do I'll keep you safe."

He obviously meant the words to be comforting, and while she knew he was capable of keeping her safe allowing him to protect her was only going to wind up breaking her heart, and it was already in pretty bad shape. "No," she said firmly.

Abe narrowed his eyes at her. "What do you mean, no?"

"I mean that I don't need your help or your protection."

"You think you can take your husband yourself? I know I don't have to tell you that he's a very dangerous man, we both know that if he gets his hands on you, he's going to punish you for running."

"Like you care," she said, her voice rising as she shoved him away from her. "You don't care about me, and I'm not going to be anyone's charity project. You can't keep me here, if you try I'll just wait and leave the second you're not looking."

Abe stood and stalked across the room, growling as he raked his hands through his hair. When he spun around to face her again his eyes were sparkling with fire. "I care about you."

That she hadn't been expecting to hear. "W-what?"

"You're not a charity project."

"Then what am I?"

A mess of emotions flashed across his face, but when he spoke his voice was even. "I don't know, but I do know that I care about you and I'm not letting that psychopath get his hands on you.

With that, he crossed the room in two large strides, grabbed her, and pulled her out of the chair, then his mouth descended on hers and he was kissing her like she was the most beautiful woman he had ever touched.

For a second she stiffened, wondering if this was a ploy to try to keep her from making good on her threat to run, but then she was yanked up against his rock hard body, and she melted into the kiss.

* * * * *

3:26 A.M.

He was kissing her.

This had to be the worst idea ever.

Only Meadow thought that she didn't mean anything to him, that she was just a burden that he wanted to fix so he could get rid of it, and he couldn't let her think that. She'd spent her whole life alone, and all she wanted was someone to care about her. Well she had that now and he wanted her to know it.

Reluctantly, he tore his mouth away from hers, he couldn't stand here kissing her all night, Julian was on the way here, and they had to pack and get out of here before her husband decided to come back. They had to find out everything they could about John Smith so they could try to figure out what his next move would be and get ahead of him.

"Wh-what are you doing?" Meadow stammered her chest heaving, her pretty sky blue eyes glistening with desire but also full of confusion.

Abe raked his hands through his hair and walked a few steps away so he could clear his head, he couldn't think straight when he was this close to her. What *was* he doing?

Developing feelings for a woman he barely knew, after he had sworn off women after Talia. He'd promised himself he would never get emotionally invested like that again. Casual dating was one thing, but there would be no falling in love, no dreaming of a future, no doing anything that left him wide open to being crushed.

And yet despite all of that, along came Meadow with her sweet nature and her baby blues, pregnant and alone and in need, making him feel things that he didn't want to be feeling.

Only now, standing here looking at Meadow, the taste of her still lingering on his lips, he wasn't sure he would change these brewing feelings even if he could.

"Did you just kiss me to try to convince me not to leave?" Meadow asked, suspicion growing on her face.

"No."

"Then why? Why did you say you care about me? Last night I cooked you dinner and you told me that the kiss we shared was a mistake. I don't understand what's changed. I don't understand ..." she trailed off as she apparently decided on an appropriate way to finish that sentence, "you."

Well that made two of them.

He wasn't sure that he could explain what was going on inside his head, but it was evident that Meadow needed some sort of explanation so he was going to have to try.

"What happened with Talia, it kind of turned me off the whole falling in love thing. I've been on my own ever since and I promised myself that I would never allow another person to have that kind of power over me. And then you came along and ... I don't know, but I do know that I like you and I care about you, and I don't want to see you get hurt. I'm sorry, I can't offer you anything more at the moment, but I can promise you that I will help you, that I won't let your husband hurt you again." He paused and dragged in a breath, he knew he wasn't being fair, but he needed a promise from Meadow that she wasn't going to run as soon as he turned his back. "But, Meadow, I need you to promise me that you're going to stick around. I can't help you if you run, and I don't want anything bad to happen to you."

Abe had to force himself not to hold his breath as he awaited an answer. He was the one who had been giving her mixed signals, so he had no right to expect her to promise him anything, and yet he *needed* her to.

Meadow tilted her head to the side and studied him, her eyes giving away nothing. She stared at him for so long that he was beginning to think she wasn't going to agree, but then she smiled and took a small step closer. "I won't run."

"You won't?" He couldn't help but sound surprised. He'd been sure she was going to stick with her plan to bolt as soon as he wasn't looking.

"I won't," she repeated.

He crossed the space between them in a single step and dragged her up against him, kissing her again. She responded, leaning into him and pressing her breasts up against him. Without even thinking about what he was doing, one hand curled around the back of her neck, pulling her closer, while his other hand slipped under the hem of her sweater, his fingertips brushing across her stomach.

Meadow tensed and he immediately stilled his hands.

Abe ended the kiss and pulled back so he could see her face. "Meadow, have you ever had sex with anyone other than your husband?" It wasn't that he wanted to make her uncomfortable, but if they were forging some sort of relationship here then he needed to know as much about her as he could because he didn't want to do anything that would be a trigger to her.

"I wouldn't really call what John and I did sex, it was more like him using my body for his own pleasure," she said softly, her gaze dropping to the floor.

That wasn't what he wanted. He didn't want her beating herself up over anything her husband had done to her. Grasping her chin, he gave it a firm shake. "He's a psychopath, whatever he did to you is because he's evil, not because of anything you did. And you didn't answer my question."

She squirmed uncomfortably but replied, "There was this guy while I was in high school. He liked my best friend, but she was in love with someone else, so I was the consolation prize, I lost my virginity to him, but it wasn't anything special. I guess I should be glad that I didn't give it to John. I, uh, I don't really know much about sex," she admitted, her pale cheeks turning bright red.

Scooping her into his arms, Abe sat down in the armchair he'd put her in when he'd brought her inside. Picking up the blanket he'd brought to help warm her up, which had fallen from her shoulders when he'd grabbed her and kissed her, he draped it around her shoulders. Her teeth had stopped chattering and she was no longer shaking, but her skin was still cold to the touch.

Settling her in his lap, he began to stroke her long blonde hair that hung loosely around her shoulders. "You don't have to give me details of what John did to you, but are you afraid of sex?" He didn't want to hurt or scare her, but he did want to make out with her so he wanted to know what he was up against.

"With John, yes. With … someone else, no I don't think so, not if I trust them not to hurt me," she answered him honestly.

"And do you trust me not to hurt you?"

"Yes," she whispered, and a shiver rocked through her, one that he suspected had nothing to do with the cold.

'Then close your eyes and relax," he instructed.

"Are we going to have sex now?" she asked, eyes wide.

He couldn't help but smile. "No, I thought we'd ease into things a little. Now close your eyes." Once she had, he said, "Tell me if anything that I do makes you uncomfortable and you want me to stop, okay?"

"Okay," she said breathily. It was clear she was already into this and they hadn't even started yet.

He didn't want to do anything to spook her. He wanted her to enjoy this, and for it to be special, something she would want to do again, something that would ease them into the next step when she—when *they*—were ready for that.

Because he knew that she was already comfortable with him kissing her, he touched his lips to hers as his hand resumed its spot on her stomach. His fingers on her bare skin must have tickled because she clenched, but then she relaxed and he knew she was enjoying this.

Taking his time, not wanting to go too fast because he knew this was all new for her, he let his fingers trail lazily backward and forward across her stomach, letting the kiss be the focus as he slowly moved his fingers higher. Her round, pregnant belly reminded him of the baby he had never even known existed until Talia threw it in his face that his being off in the military was the cause of the miscarriage.

But today wasn't about that.

Meadow wasn't anything like Talia, and he knew she would never do anything like that.

His fingertips brushed the underside of her breast, and he wondered whether she was going to freak out, but she didn't. A sweet little hum reverberated through her and she pressed her chest forward, silently begging for more.

Abe smiled inwardly. Maybe this whole relationship thing wasn't so bad after all.

* * * * *

3:39 A.M.

Finally.

Meadow hummed her pleasure when Abe's hand finally

claimed her breast. He tenderly massaged it, not too hard, but also not too soft, the kneading motion made heat swell in her body. Then he found her nipple and he was teasing it, rolling it between his fingertips and that heat grew, and she realized she'd never known how sensitive her nipples were.

For pleasure anyway.

She knew they were sensitive to pain.

Abe could no doubt feel the scars—from the pliers, the knives, her husband's teeth—that marred her skin, but thankfully he wasn't mentioning it, he was just allowing her to enjoy learning about all the ways a lover could bring you pleasure.

Is that what they were now?

Lovers?

They hadn't really talked about the future, but he had told her he cared about her and he'd promised to keep her safe, and she was currently snuggled in his lap while he ministered to her breasts and kissed her.

The light from a car's headlights filled the room, and she heard the rev of an engine. Just like that all the wonderful things Abe was making her feel vanished, and she froze.

John.

He must be back.

"Shh, it's okay," Abe soothed. "It's only my cousin Julian, he's going to take us down to the station while I figure out where you should stay until we get your husband in custody."

"You're sending me away?" she asked, a little bit of panic clawing at her insides.

"Yes," Abe said, but the corners of his mouth quirked up in a smile. "But I'm going with you."

"Oh." Meadow let out a relieved sigh.

"Why don't you go upstairs and pack a few things, we're not going to be back here until this is over."

Abe stood with her in his arms then set her down on her feet, pulling the blanket tighter around her shoulders. Then he leaned down and pressed a tender kiss to her forehead.

Just like that the mushy feeling in her stomach was back.

Somehow Abe possessed the ability to make her feel safe, no one else had ever done that before.

A knock sounded on the door, and since Abe didn't look concerned, she didn't worry either.

With an arm around her shoulders, he took her with him to the door, and unlocked it to let his cousin in.

"Julian, this is Meadow. Meadow, Julian," he made the introductions.

"Hi, Meadow," Julian gave her an easy smile, his hazel eyes twinkling, and she immediately felt relaxed around him.

"Hi," she smiled back.

"Run upstairs and pack, there's a suitcase in the closet," he told her, nudging her toward the staircase, and since she assumed that he needed to talk to his deputy about something work-related she did as he'd asked.

In her bedroom she found the suitcase and put the clothes Abe had gotten from his sister for her to wear and folded and packed them neatly. When she was done, she went into the bathroom to clean up. Her face was tear-stained, and the marks around her neck made her realize just how close she had come to dying tonight. John was a terrifying man, and she hated being the center of his anger.

"Ready?" Abe popped his head through the bedroom door.

"Yes."

He took the suitcase handle from her and carried it and his own bag down the stairs. They followed Julian out to the car, and once she was sitting alone in the backseat, Meadow finally realized just how serious things were. The little bubble of happiness and safety that Abe had created for her in his living room was gone now and the stark realization that she was going to have to tell them everything she knew about John was starting to sink in.

"We're here." Abe's voice broke through her thoughts, and she realized that he had opened her car door and was holding out his hand to her.

At least she didn't have to do this alone, that was one saving grace.

Meadow took Abe's hand and let him lead her into the police station. She thought that he might take her into a stark, sterile interrogation room while he peppered her with questions, but he didn't, he led her into his office and over to a leather couch in the corner.

"You want something to drink?" he asked.

She was way too nervous for that. "I just want to get this over and done with."

Again she had expected that Abe would take a seat across from her, he was the cop in this situation, and she was the witness or victim or whatever it was he saw her as. But he didn't do that, he sat beside her and took her hand in his, holding it tightly enough that she knew she wasn't alone.

"So while you were upstairs packing, Julian told me some things he found out about your husband," Abe began, his voice a lot more gentle than she thought it probably was when he spoke with anyone else.

"Oh," she said because she wasn't sure what else to say.

"Your husband killed a teenager, left her in a car with a whole bunch of flowers. A meadow," he added.

"He stuck a knife inside her and slit her open from vagina to breasts," she murmured more to herself than to Abe or Julian.

"How did you know that?" Abe asked.

She couldn't help the shudder that ripped through her. "Because John told me it was what he would do to me if I ever left him." Actually, he had been a lot more descriptive, going into great detail about how much he would enjoy shoving the blade of a knife inside her vagina and then slicing slowly through her body, cutting her open from the inside out. Shame burned inside her making her cheeks flame red and her eyes sting, she had been the weak, pathetic victim for too long. John had stolen her power, convinced her that she was nothing and she had believed him. But not anymore, she was going to find a way to get her power back.

"It's okay," Abe soothed, wrapping an arm around her shoulders. "I'm not ever going to let him do that to you, sweetheart."

Meadow froze.

Sweetheart.

She began to shake in earnest now as memories began to assault her at a faster pace than she could handle.

The world began to spin around her like it had suddenly decided a trip to the amusement park was in order, only neither her head nor her stomach agreed.

Lips touched her forehead.

Their warmth seemed to seep into her ice-cold body.

Abe had pulled her onto his lap and was cradling her, rocking her from side to side, his arms like steel bands around her making her feel protected, cocooned in a little bubble of strong muscles.

"Sunshine, what's wrong?"

Sunshine.

That was better.

That was what she had become accustomed to him calling her.

"Sunshine, what happened? What freaked you out?"

"Sweetheart," she murmured, her mouth feeling like it was burning just ripping the word from her lips. "John used to call me that. I used to think it was because of my name. He liked flowers, he would beat me if I let any of the bushes he planted in the garden die, or if he brought me flowers and they died."

"That's what flowers do, he was setting you up to fail." Abe sounded angry, and while it touched her to know that he was angry for her it didn't change anything.

"John didn't care. He liked to hurt me. When he had me in the bedroom he used to like to go between my legs, tell me that I smelled beautiful, I thought in his warped head my name made him think of a meadow of flowers, but when you called me sweetheart just now I think maybe I was wrong."

"Why do you think you were wrong?" Julian asked.

"Baking. It's because I bake. The night that he proposed we were having dinner at my apartment, and I baked this apple crumble, the recipe was his mother's. She had died when he was just a kid, and he talked about her all the time. Maybe that's why he always stopped short of killing me. I could bake like his mother."

"Meadow," Abe said slowly, and she knew she wasn't going to like what he said next. "His mother isn't dead, she's in a psychiatric hospital. She had a breakdown after she was accused of sexually abusing him. But Julian and I were talking. John is a manipulator, and he's violent, he takes pleasure in hurting others. The woman in the car that we found yesterday, she wasn't the first killed that way, there have been over a dozen women killed that same exact way."

Over a dozen women killed the exact same way her husband had threatened to kill her, all left in a meadow of flowers?

Her husband wasn't just abusive, he was a serial killer.

She was married to a serial killer.

With a quiet sob she sunk down against Abe and buried her face against his chest. She felt like such a fool. How could she not have seen it?

How could she not know she was living with a killer?

Carrying a killer's baby inside her.

Meadow wasn't sure her life could get any worse.

* * * * *

6:44 A.M.

John was annoyed.

He was annoyed that his wife had run.

139

He was annoyed that he had to come and find her and drag her back.

He was annoyed that he'd been interrupted when he'd run her car off the road.

He was annoyed that the sheriff had interrupted him tonight when he had Meadow in his grasp.

He was annoyed that now he had to waste more time finding out where she was and how he would get to her.

He was annoyed that thanks to her no doubt opening her mouth and telling the cops his name, he could no longer go back to his old life.

Thankfully, being who he was he had always been prepared for the possibility that one day everything would come crashing down around him, and he would have to make a quick getaway, and as soon as Meadow had run he had begun getting ready to disappear. He had plenty of cash, had a property in another name where he could stay, and had a new identity ready to use, but it was still annoying that he would have to give up his old life.

Since he couldn't change those facts he was going to accept it. Getting Meadow home—to their new home—where she belonged, punishing her for her ridiculous running away antics which made her look more like a bratty teenager than a woman in her twenties, definitely soothed some of his anger.

It would be so much easier to cut his losses, let her go and find someone else, but he never let go of what was his.

Never.

Maybe if Meadow hadn't been carrying his baby it would have been easier to let her go, but that child was his, he was the father, and she had no right to run and take his baby with her.

As angry as he was with her, he was going to have to show some measure of restraint when he did get her back. Since she was pregnant and since he did want his child, he couldn't very well beat her into oblivion or he'd risk losing the baby. Not that that meant she was getting off scot-free because she definitely was not. She would be punished, and he was already dreaming up all the ways he would do it. By the time he was done, she would think twice before ever deciding to disobey him.

If it wasn't for the baby he would probably have killed her for her insolence, but now he needed her, and not just to carry the fetus to term but also to care for it once it was born. He might view this child as his legacy, but that didn't mean he would be changing diapers, giving bottles, and getting up to tend to a screaming infant in the middle of the night. That wasn't his cup of tea. So he would need to keep Meadow alive at least until the child was weaned and able to care for its own needs.

While he might be planning on keeping her alive he wouldn't be allowing her to roam free. He would keep her locked away, her sole purpose in life to care for their child. He'd feed her just enough food and give her just enough water to keep her alive. And maybe he would bring her in on his … side activity.

John couldn't help but smile as he thought of his hobby. He had no idea how Meadow had never caught on, perhaps it was because she was too afraid of him to spend her time doing anything but trying to avoid making him angry.

Which let's face it, was impossible.

Deep seeded anger had plagued him for as long as he could remember.

As a child he had gotten into fights at school, he had ruled his classroom with an iron fist, the teachers and the other children were afraid of him, and he grew to relish that fear.

Fear was life.

Without it he was nothing but an angry man.

But so long as he could channel that anger into causing fear in others, it felt like his life served a purpose.

Even as a man quickly approaching forty, he was able to instill fear in others. He supposed his job had something to do with it, his ruthless nature and enjoyment of others suffering made him perfectly suited for his career of choice, and while he didn't really think anyone would ever suspect him of beating his wife let alone being a serial killer, he was sure if the truth eventually came out that no one would be particularly surprised.

The sheriff of this little town obviously had his claws into Meadow, and he had no doubt that the man would persuade her to tell him everything, but that didn't mean that the cops would be able to find him. The new house was secure, he had cashed in all his stocks and bonds, and that added to the cash he hoarded in the safe in his house was enough to keep him living comfortably for many years to come. And once he had Meadow and his baby back he could focus on them for a while, then when the timing was right, he could forge a new life.

One that definitely included more victims.

John knew he was lucky that Meadow was as gullible as she was. And not just Meadow, every single one of his victims had willingly come walking right into his trap, he'd never committed an abduction in his life.

But never say never.

Last night when that stupid sheriff had stopped him just moments before he had been ready to pull Meadow into his car and take her home, he had threatened to keep killing people in the man's town if he got in the way of his business. The sheriff had gotten in the middle of his relationship, and since he was a man of his word, he was going to follow through on his threat.

Since there was obviously no time to woo his potential victim the way he usually would, he was going to have to go the abduction route, which was surprisingly exciting. Usually, he was a guy who liked routine, he liked structure, it was the only way he could keep the angry beast inside him leashed and under control. But this morning he would be throwing caution to the wind and grabbing the first young woman he saw.

The temptation to circle back around to the sheriff's house had been strong, but he had fought against it because he knew that no doubt the man had moved Meadow already and left someone else in the house who would arrest him if he returned. So since that was out, he decided that staking out the town's park was his best bet. He was sure that sooner or later some pretty young thing was going to come for a jog. All he had to do was wait and then grab her when she got close enough.

John was a confident guy, and he wasn't really worried that things wouldn't work out the way he wanted them to. Things *always* worked out the way he wanted them to. It was just the way his life went, well, until Meadow decided to mess things up by running.

He still couldn't believe she had done it.

She had always been so pliant, so desperate for love, and to no longer be alone that she had all but thrown herself at him. They had been together now for five years, and all that time, no matter what he did to her, she never talked back, and she never fought back because in the end she knew that he was the only one who was ever going to want her. And in some warped way he *did* actually love her. Not enough that he was ever going to stop hurting her, but he had become accustomed to her presence. She was the only one he had ever spent so much time with, all the other women he conned he kept alive only for a couple of days while he got his fill of torturing them before he killed them and moved on to the next.

There.

Up ahead.

Someone was running toward him.

He looked closer and saw a young woman, maybe late teens or early twenties, his favorite age.

John started jogging.

He usually went to the gym and lifted weights, so he hoped he looked enough like a jogger than she assumed he was one and didn't perceive him as a threat.

She was getting closer. Not even looking at him, she had earphones in and seemed lost in whatever she was listening to.

They approached each other.

They passed each other.

Then just as he was a step or two past her, he pounced.

Spinning around, he grabbed hold of the girl and yanked her up against his chest, simultaneously clamping a hand over her mouth so she couldn't scream and alert anyone who might be nearby.

The girl thrashed in his grip, but she was a tiny little thing, much smaller than him, and he easily dragged her into the trees where they would be less likely to be seen as he headed for his car. Once he got there he would gag her, blindfold her, and bind her wrists and ankles before stuffing her in the trunk and driving her to the motel he was staying in.

For a first abduction he had to say, he would give himself a perfect score.

* * * * *

10:53 A.M.

She looked so peaceful in her sleep.

Meadow was curled up on the couch in his office. It had taken him a while to convince her to lie down for a bit and try to get some rest, she'd been exhausted from reliving the hell her husband had put her through but also wired, edgy, and terrified, and sleep was the last thing on her mind. Because he knew she needed it he had insisted, suggesting that she lie down here in his office where he could keep an eye on her, and she would know she wasn't alone. After a lot of persuasion, she had relented and agreed, and he was pretty sure she had passed out within a minute of her head hitting the pillow.

She was doing her best to hold it together, and she was doing a better job at it than Abe thought she realized, but still he had to wonder how long that could last.

Especially if her husband followed through on his threats to start killing the residents of River's End if they prevented him from getting his wife back.

Not that that changed anything.

He was the sheriff, it was his job to protect the people, but he couldn't exchange one life for another, particularly if that one life was Meadow's.

There was no point in denying that he liked her. Kissing her and touching her, he knew that she wasn't just some woman he wanted to help because she didn't have anyone else.

She was special.

She was special to him.

He wasn't ready to jump headfirst into a relationship. He wanted to take things slowly, and given that she was pregnant with another man's baby and dealing with her serial killer abusive husband, he doubted Meadow was in any hurry to rush things either. But he did want to get to know her, spend time with her, let her get to know him, definitely do a lot more making out, and then maybe they would find that they wanted to make a permanent commitment to spend the rest of their lives together.

Meadow was his now, even if they were going to take this burgeoning relationship slowly, and nobody messed with what was his, so he would just have to hope that they were able to find John Smith before he got a chance to go after anyone else.

"Hey," Julian said softly, opening the door to his office and quietly walking in. "She still out?"

"Yeah," he replied, finally tearing his eyes from Meadow's sleeping face. With her blonde hair fanned out around her porcelain pale skin she looked like an angel. *His* angel. So he better stop staring at her like some hormone ravaged teenager and start working on finding her husband. "Let's talk out here so we don't disturb her."

As much as he wanted to not let Meadow out of his sight, he had a job to do, and he intended to do it. Abe followed Julian out into the hall and into the other office. The River's End police station was small, with two offices, the smaller of which was his and the larger one shared by his deputies, a foyer, two interview rooms, and a row of four cells they usually used as a drunk tank but also for the occasional burglar, or hit and run driver, drug dealer, or petty thief. In all his years in River's End, he didn't think a murderer had ever been kept in one of those cells, but now he was imagining Meadow's husband sitting in one, and he couldn't help but smile at the image. Behind bars was too good a place for a man who had done the things John Smith had, but it would have to suffice. Unless of course the man wouldn't go quietly, then he might find himself in a body bag, and Abe liked that idea so much better.

"John Smith is a prominent defense attorney, responsible for getting dozens of murderers and rapists acquitted, leaving them free to roam the streets," Julian told him when they walked into the other office and took seats at the desk. "I told the local cops what we know, and asked them to go and pick him up, but he had packed up the house, and it's clear he's in the wind."

Abe muttered a curse under his breath. They knew the guy was in River's End, but he had been hoping that at some point he intended to return home, where he would be immediately arrested, but that didn't look like it was going to happen. While they had their killer's identity, they didn't know where he was which meant they would have to work off their profile of John Smith based on his crimes and what Meadow knew about him. Abe prayed would be enough to find him.

"What did you get on the other murders?" he asked. When Julian had arrived at his house in the early hours of the morning to pick him and Meadow up and bring them here, he'd sent her upstairs to pack so he could check in with his cousin and see what he had found out so far. When he had learned that Meadow's husband was not just abusive but also likely a serial killer, he had known that things were a lot more dangerous than he had realized.

"Fifteen murders all where the woman was found cut from the vagina to breasts, left surrounded by hundreds of flowers. The murders are spread over the last five years—looks like they started not long after he married Meadow—and he dumps the bodies in different locations. Kills them where he leaves them, that was the determination based on the amount of blood at the scenes. Obvious evidence of torture on all the victims, both physical and sexual, all had been missing for between two and five days with the exception of our victim, and all were college students. Families and friends all reported the same things; the victims had been enamored with an older man and believed they were in love, they all went to this guy willingly. He's obviously charismatic enough to lure them in without having to abduct them outright. He's smart enough not to leave behind any forensics that point to him, and so far the cops have no suspects. Until now anyway," Julian added.

"He's angry, whether about this supposed sexual abuse by his mother or something else, or it's just who he is, he has anger that he needs to find a way to satiate so it doesn't consume him. That's why he needed Meadow. He needed to have someone there whenever he felt the urge to take out his aggression on someone. The others are more for fun. It's like his hobby, the game of luring them in, convincing them to come to him willingly, that stokes his ego, then he enjoys torturing them until he loses interest and murders them."

"I was thinking about what Meadow told us earlier, about how much he loves flowers and how he would get angry if she let one of the bushes die. We know that he takes a souvenir from each of his victims and I was wondering whether he buries it beneath the bushes. We should ask Meadow, see if she remembers dates of when the bushes were planted, and we can ask CSU to check out the yard, see if we're right and he does bury his souvenirs there."

The souvenirs they were talking about were actually his

victims' breasts which he cut off once he had cut them virtually in half. It was an interesting theory, and one he was sure could be easily confirmed, but right now what was worrying him more was how John Smith knew that Meadow was in River's End. "How did he find her here?"

"She said she paid cash for the ticket so no way he could have traced it, and River's End isn't the kind of place you'd think you'd stop and look for the wife you abuse," Julian agreed. "You think he used a tracking device?"

That was exactly what he had been thinking. John had known exactly where to come looking for his wife down to the car she had been driving and the house she had been staying in. "She didn't bring much with her when she left, no cell phone or anything, just the clothes on her back."

Julian's eyes grew wide. "You think the tracker is in *her*?"

"I think that we should take a trip to visit Levi and have him check her out," he said grimly. The idea of John putting a tracker in Meadow, no doubt without her consent, made his blood boil. To John, Meadow was just like a pet that you didn't want to lose, she wasn't a person, she was his toy who he liked to play with.

Before he could say more, the door opened, and a bleak-looking Fletcher walked in. "We may have a situation."

"A situation?" he repeated, not liking the sound of that. Since he knew that Meadow was safe here it had to mean that John Smith had followed through on his threats.

"Darlene Frindlebrook is missing. She went out jogging this morning then was supposed to go straight to her classes, but she never showed up, her car is still parked at the park, no sign of her anywhere," Fletcher explained.

He knew where Darlene was, she was with John, she was his next victim, and unless they found her, he knew exactly what was going to happen to her. Fighting his instincts, which were to stay here with Meadow and keep her safe since she was what John really wanted, he sighed and stood up. He was the sheriff, and he had to go to the scene, speak with any witnesses, inform the family, who he had known since he was a kid, and do whatever he could to find Darlene.

"Julian, stay here with Meadow, don't let her out of your sight for any reason. Call Levi and tell him that he needs to check Meadow for any tracking devices. Fletcher, you're with me," he barked out as he stalked from the room, ready to rip John Smith to shreds with his bare hands when he finally tracked the man down.

* * * * *

6:36 P.M.

It had been a really long day.

Meadow wanted Abe to come back, but she knew he was busy, working hard trying to find her husband before he had a chance to come for her again.

While she appreciated that—in words she could never fully express—she knew how dangerous it was, and she was terrified that John would hurt Abe. Well, not just hurt him, more like torture and kill him. John wouldn't let anyone get in the way of him getting her back, and Abe had planted himself directly in the line of fire. It meant John would do whatever it took to eliminate him.

According to what Abe and his cousin Julian had told her, John had been killing women for five years now. The whole time she had been married to him, living with him, sleeping beside him, cooking and cleaning for him, doing his laundry, he had been seducing teenage girls and slaughtering them. They hadn't had to tell her that he'd tortured them for her to know that he had. He'd tortured her so it stood to reason that he would have done the same things to them he had done to her for five long years.

None of it had sunk in yet.

She felt like she was living someone else's life.

Any second now, she would wake up and find out she hadn't been tricked into marrying a serial killer.

A *serial killer.*

She hadn't even known that serial killers got married, but what had she known? She was a nineteen-year-old kid, starved for love and attention, desperate for anyone to give her a scrap of love.

Now shame filled her. She felt responsible for John's actions, she had probably washed the clothes—stained with his victims' blood—that he had worn while he killed them. The thought made her sick. Had he raped them and then come home and raped her?

A hand touched her shoulder, and she shrieked.

"It's only me."

She spun around and saw Abe standing behind her. She blushed, embarrassed by freaking out in front of him again. As if it wasn't enough that she had sobbed all over him when she learned the truth about John, and then been a hysterical mess for hours while he wasted time calming her down that could have been better spent trying to find John.

"I wasn't sure I was going to see you again today," she said, trying to calm herself down. While she had paced back and forth across Abe's office all day, too stressed to settle at anything, she'd decided that she wasn't going to be the poor, beaten down, abused wife anymore. She was going to be strong, she was going to be tough, she was going to be independent, she was going to take care of herself, after all, she had made it through eighteen years of foster care on her own.

"Of course you were going to see me again today," he told her.

She wasn't sure what to do. Meadow still wasn't one hundred percent certain of where things stood between them. Yes, he had told her that he had feelings for her and that he would be there for her, they'd made out, and he'd held her while she cried. But did that make them a couple?

Tentatively, she lifted her eyes to meet his, he was watching her, an inscrutable expression on his face. Then he curled an arm around her waist, drew her close, and touched his lips to hers in a soft, sweet kiss.

"Dinner?" he asked.

Her eyes widened. "Like a date?"

"Yes, a date. I thought we could go out to dinner, and then we're spending the night at my brother Theo's house. He's on shift at the fire station so we have the place to ourselves."

Those words hung over her, making her tingle in all the right places. She'd thought after everything John had done to her she would never be able to think of sex as a pleasurable thing, but Abe made her want to strip naked and let his hands and his mouth touch her all over, then bury himself inside her and make her come, screaming his name.

"Shall we go?"

A delightful shiver rocked through her, and she nodded, taking the hand that he held out. The idea of going out on a date was exciting, and she wondered what he had planned. "So where are we going?" she asked as he led her through the station, pausing at the door to help her put on her coat.

"There's an amazing pizzeria on Main Street, I thought we'd go there, then to the ice cream parlor, and Theo's house is in town so we can walk there after we're done."

"That sounds wonderful," she said with a smile, actually she couldn't stop smiling. When she had run from John she hadn't been expecting to meet someone that she would even think about having a future with. She'd run for her the sake of her baby because she couldn't condemn a child to the life she had been living, but she hadn't really expected to build a new life.

"Do you want to drive to the pizzeria or walk? It's only about a ten-minute walk, but it's meant to snow later."

"Let's walk, it's so beautiful out here." It was dark out, but the lights of the town were winking on, and she knew that Main Street was lined with streetlights and fairy lights. It made the town look so pretty.

It was fate that had brought her here.

It had to be.

How else could you explain it?

She had been scrounging money ever since she learned she was pregnant and the amount she had managed to save was just enough to get her a bus ticket here. Here to this adorable little town where the man who was quickly becoming very important to her lived.

"What are you thinking about?" Abe asked, breaking the companionable silence.

"About how lucky I am."

"Lucky?"

"I'm alive, aren't I? All of John's other victims aren't, and now I'm here, with you, and we're going on a date, and later we're going to do a little kissing."

"Oh, we're going to do a lot more than a little kissing," he whispered in her ear, making her shiver.

A delightful shiver.

Her dark world was finally starting to fill with light.

Something that Meadow had been so sure was never going to happen.

Now she was excited about what her future held. Once the threat of John was no longer hanging over her head, she would finally be able to live.

Really live, and it was such an exhilarating prospect.

It made her want to sing and dance and laugh and throw caution to the wind. She wanted to feel part of the real world after being a prisoner for so long, she wanted to just enjoy herself for once.

"Can we have ice cream first?" she asked as they walked past the ice cream parlor.

Abe shot her an amused smile. "Sure, if you want. Do you want to go in and have sundaes, or do you want to grab cones and we can sit out here?"

"Out here," she replied immediately. She wanted to enjoy the chilly evening.

"What flavor do you want?"

"Surprise me."

"Okeydokey."

"Okeydokey?" she snickered at the word that totally didn't seem like something Abe would say.

He shrugged and smiled. "Just wanted to make you smile, when you do it lights up your eyes, and your whole face is transformed."

His sweet words did indeed make her smile, and she watched him walk into the ice cream parlor. For all his attempts and pretending he was this strong macho guy, he was like a big squishable teddy bear inside.

Snow began to flutter around her, and she squealed in excitement. Besides tending the garden and the occasional trip out to functions with John, Meadow couldn't remember the last time she had been outside just to have fun. With a giggle, she stepped out into the quiet street and began to spin in circles as snowflakes fell around her. She didn't care that people were looking at her, she didn't care that the gossip mill in the small town would have word spread to everyone about the crazy new pregnant lady playing in the snow like a child.

"What are you doing?" Abe asked, two ice cream cones in his hand, watching her with a bemused expression.

"It's snowing," she squealed.

"I can see that. Again though, what are you doing?"

"Playing in the snow. Oh," she stopped spinning to clap her hands delightedly, "if we get enough snow we can make snow angels. Ooh, and a snowman. I always wanted to build a really big snowman, as big as me. Wouldn't that be fun?"

"Not as fun as this." Balancing the two cones in one hand, Abe wrapped an arm around her waist, lifted her feet off the ground, and kissed her like he thought she was every bit as beautiful as the magical world around them.

"This is pretty fun," she agreed.

"Can we eat our ice cream now?" he asked with a small pout that made her giggle.

"I guess. What flavor did you get?" she asked as he set her back on her feet, but kept a warm arm around her.

"Mint chocolate chip," he replied, handing her a cone.

"Oh, that's my favorite," she beamed.

"It's mine too," Abe agreed. "Well it used to be, I think I have a new favorite now," he whispered in her ear, and that shiver was back.

This really was the most perfect first date ever, and yet she couldn't wait for it to be over so they could go back to Abe's brother's house and fool around.

* * * * *

8:18 P.M.

Given everything she had been through, Meadow was surprisingly resilient. She'd chattered away, laughing and making jokes, her body responded every time he touched her, and Abe knew that she was every bit as anxious as he was to get back to his brother's house so they could do more than kiss and hold hands. He couldn't be more proud of her. What she had lived through was horrific, add to that what her childhood had been like and knowing her mother hadn't wanted her after her father's death, and he thought she was perhaps the bravest woman he had ever met.

Strike that, quite possibly the bravest *person* he had ever met.

Maybe it was precisely the difficult childhood and situation with her parents that had helped her survive her marriage.

Meadow had been used to being on her own, she had been

154

used to being unwanted, and she was used to pain, albeit emotional and psychological pain. The sweet, funny, lively, bubbly, carefree woman that she would have been had life not handed her a series of blows had not been trampled down, she was still in there, and now that she had been set free that woman was soaring.

She'd fallen quiet now though, they'd had their ice cream, they'd had dinner, they'd gathered up the small amount of snow that had built up on the ground and made the world's tiniest snowman. Now they were heading back to his brother's house, and he was wondering if now the reality of being with another man—whatever they ended up doing and the ball was firmly in her court—was catching up with her.

"Everything okay," he asked, his thumb brushing across her knuckles.

"Yes," she replied, but her voice was troubled.

"Doesn't sound like it."

Meadow sighed and stopped walking, looking up at him with anxious eyes. "Do you think there's something wrong with me?"

"Wrong with you?" He might not date a lot, but he knew a loaded question when he heard one. There was no good answer he could give to that because it was clear she thought there was something wrong with herself. "What do you mean?"

"I feel happy."

"What's the problem with that?" Abe asked, thoroughly confused, he'd forgotten how much women baffled him.

"I've spent the last five years married to a man who beat and raped me nearly every day, he's still out there, and he's made it clear he intends to get me back." Her free hand strayed to her neck as she said those words, and the hand-shaped bruises there reminded him just how close John Smith had gotten to getting his wish. "It seems like I should be cowering in a corner in terror, a complete and utter mess, and yet here I am, out on a date, holding your hand and picturing all the things those fingers are going to do when we get to your brother's house. It seems … wrong?"

"You finally feel safe to be you. The real you." Meadow apparently saw her strength as a weakness which had to be the mother of all ironies.

"I do feel safe with you," she said, but her voice sounded odd. Like that was somehow a bad thing. "I have a confession to make. When I cooked you that dinner last night, it was to try to get you to like me, you know *like* like me."

"I know," he said, brushing his fingers across her cheek.

"But my motives were wrong. I didn't want you to like me because I liked you, I wanted you to like me because I thought I needed you."

He froze.

His hand dropped to his side.

Was she trying to tell him that she wasn't interested in him after all?

That would have to be the father of all ironies because he had spent the last decade of his life using women to fulfill his needs, knowing he had nothing of substance to offer them. Now he'd found a woman who made him want to dig down deep inside himself and find more to offer, and she didn't want him.

"I'm not explaining it right," Meadow said anxiously. "Last night I thought that I needed someone like you to take care of me. You're strong, and tough, and big, and you made me feel safe, and I didn't think I could survive on my own. For the last five years, John has told me every opportunity that he got that I'm weak, and pathetic, that I couldn't survive on my own, that I needed a man to look after me and that's why I would never leave him. You hear that often enough and you believe it. But when you told me the kiss was a mistake it hurt and I realized that I was starting to care for you. *Really* care for you. When I was upstairs waiting for you to fall asleep so I could sneak away, I realized that deep down inside you're scared too. You're scared of getting hurt, that the next woman you fall in love with will turn out to be like your ex, so you push everyone away, you don't let them get close. But you didn't let those fears stop you from being there for me. You held me while I cried, you made me feel for the first time in my life that I mattered. Then you touched me, and my body felt alive, I've never felt desirable or attractive before, but you make me feel that way." Tugging her hand free from his, she pressed both to his chest and stood on her tiptoes to whisper her lips across his. "Take me home and make my heart come alive by making love to me."

Abe was stunned by Meadow's beautiful words and her insightful views on both herself and him.

Talia *had* made him afraid to try loving someone again, but Meadow's sweetness, and somewhat shaky determination to build a new life for herself and her baby, touched something deep down inside him. If she could endure everything life had thrown at her and still hold out hope that something better was waiting for her right around the next corner, then maybe he could let go of his fears too. Accept that life didn't have to be a chore, that happiness really could be waiting for him out there, most likely all wrapped up in a five-foot three-inch frame, topped with hair that reminded him of sunshine, and eyes that were bluer than a summer sky.

"Are you sure?" he asked. He hadn't been expecting that she would be ready for sex. He'd thought they'd just make out a little then go to sleep holding each other in their arms.

"I have never been surer of anything in my life." Her confidence faltered a little. "Unless you don't want to."

"Baby, I want to," he said with a growl. Scooping her up into his arms, ignoring any of the town busybodies who were no doubt watching and would no doubt have the rumor mill running rampant by sunrise, he all but ran the last block and a half to his brother's house.

Balancing Meadow in one arm, he nibbled at her neck as he pulled his keys from his pocket and let them inside. Intending to carry her upstairs to the bedroom, he stopped when Meadow said, "Here, now, please, I need you inside me. I want to feel you, I want you to be a part of me. I don't want you to treat me like I'm going to break and go slow. I want you to claim me, own me."

Never one to turn down a woman who was begging him to own her, he set Meadow on her feet and ripped her pants and panties down her legs. "Next time we go the slow route because I want to touch and taste every inch of your beautiful body," he murmured in her ear.

Desire heated her face and her cheeks turned pink. "I can't wait."

Picking her up again, he sat her on the edge of the dining room table, his fingers touching her, finding her more than ready for him, as she shoved his jeans and boxers down his legs. He pulled a condom from his pocket and quickly donned it, then gently pressed on her shoulders, laying her back so he could get better access without her beautiful pregnant stomach in the way. Abe nudged her legs further apart and stood between them.

Pushing a finger inside her he stroked her, teasing her, tempting her with what was coming, then added another, stretching her, preparing her. She moaned, and he could feel her quivering around his fingers, already so close. He wondered if she had ever had an orgasm before because if she hadn't, she was about to get the shock of her life.

"Watch me, Meadow," he ordered. "Don't take your eyes off me, this is how it's supposed to be, how it's supposed to feel."

Obediently, she propped herself up on her elbows and locked her eyes on his. She gasped as he entered her in one swift movement and he would have asked if he'd hurt her if he couldn't see the pleasure written all over her pretty face.

He began to move, slowly at first, he was already hard and about to come, but he wanted to make sure that they hit that peak of bliss together.

"Faster, Abe, harder," Meadow begged, her hips moving to

meet each one of his thrusts.

He couldn't say no to a lady, so he increased the speed, drawing back so he was almost out of her, then pushing back in until she took every inch of him inside her.

She was moaning, shaking, begging for more, and he could see she was teetering right on the edge. He reached between them and touched her, and she screamed his name, the clenching of her internal muscles as her orgasm hit was enough to make him come, and they rode the wave of pleasure together.

"Oh, my," Meadow panted when she finally floated back down to earth. "That was … I don't even have words." Tears glistened in her eyes and she sat up, reaching for his hands. "Abe, that was … that was perfect. I've never done that before, thank you, thank you for making me feel like a real person, thank you for making me feel special and wanted."

"It was no hardship, sunshine," he drawled as he pulled out of her and tossed the condom in the bin in the corner. "Now we get to do things a little slower, and I get to taste every inch of this delectable body."

He knelt between her legs, and when his tongue touched her, she quivered and moaned, and he knew that it was going to be a long time before they fell asleep in each other's arms because there was so much he wanted to show her about how things should be.

* * * * *

8:57 P.M.

Disgusting.

Watching another man put his mouth on his wife's most intimate area made him want to throw up.

John had never been so angry in his life.

Sure, he had an anger problem, but this was something else, he was literally seeing red, and he was shaking all over, his hands were curled into fists so tightly that his nails—trimmed short as they were—were digging into the flesh of his palms.

How dare he.

How dare *she*.

What had happened to his quiet, submissive Meadow, the woman who was too terrified to take a breath without his permission? All those years of training, only allowing her to go to the bathroom when he told her she could, eating what and when he allowed, beating out of her any fight she may have had, and in just a couple of days all of that had been undone.

Meadow was having an affair.

Okay, so he had deliberately targeted her, sensing the grating need inside her to be wanted, and lured her in, never intending to marry her, simply torture and then kill her like he had done with all the others, but then she'd cooked that meal for him, and before he knew it he had been proposing. The idea of keeping a live victim, ready and waiting for him whenever he wanted her, hadn't occurred to him until he realized that Meadow could serve that purpose. And served her purpose she had. He'd thought she was the dutiful wife, but here she was having sex with a stranger and letting him put his mouth and his hands on her.

Even through the closed window, he could hear her moans and her scream as she came. She'd never done that with him, of course he had never given her anything to scream about, nothing pleasurable anyway, her pleasure hadn't been important to him.

Nor was it important to him now.

He wanted her back because she belonged to him and he would never share her with any other man.

With a guttural growl rumbling low in his chest, he turned and slunk away. If he stayed here any longer, he would do something that would get him either killed or thrown in prison, and neither of those options sounded particularly pleasant.

For now, John knew where Meadow was, and that would have

to be enough for the moment. If they decided to move her, he would follow her there too, but he didn't intend to leave things that long. He was going to go back to the motel and then he was going to set up a diversion. As soon as the cops all went running off, leaving Meadow alone, he was going to get her.

Already he was vibrating with the need to punish her.

It was going to be so sweet, so delicious, he could hardly wait.

But he did have to wait.

Because waiting and planning meant things went according to plan. He hadn't killed fifteen—now seventeen and soon to be eighteen—people over the last five years and got away with it because he made stupid, rash, spur of the moment decisions.

So back to the motel it was. Since he'd known that Meadow was tucked away at the police station where he couldn't get to her, he had spent the day enjoying playing with his new toy. He didn't know her name and he didn't care to. She was serving a different purpose than the rest of the girls he had claimed, so he was okay with killing her now even if he had intended to keep her a little longer.

He'd thought it might be fun for Meadow to watch while he hurt the other woman, since his wife suddenly had such an urge to insert herself into his business he'd let her. Maybe he would take another woman and let her watch as he raped her, as he beat her, as he did all the things to her he had done to Meadow. Then she'd see just how lucky she was that he had kept her alive.

She should be dead right now.

Buried in his backyard beneath a rose bush just like all the others.

Well just like *part* of the others.

Instead, Meadow was alive and for that she should be getting down on her knees and kissing his shoes in thanks, not taking advantage of his generosity and tattling on him to the cops and having sex with them.

Jumping the fence and walking through the yard of the house

beside the one that Meadow and her sheriff were shacked up in, he continued jumping fences until he got to the last house on the block and ended up back on the street. River's End was small, and it wasn't late, there were people still out and about, but he wasn't worried about anyone noticing him. He was good at being a shadow, while he lived his life in the public eye, taking on the most high profile cases he could, he hid the monster inside him because it was necessary for his survival. When the need dictated, he knew how to make himself invisible, and right now, he slinked through the streets to the car he had stolen earlier.

Although he wanted to speed, he stuck precisely to the speed limit as he headed back to the motel just outside of River's End. It wasn't as nice as the hotel where Meadow had been working the last couple of days, but this one had cabins that were separated from each other so he had a little privacy. No one had known he was there with Carla Briscoe so he had stayed here even after committing the two murders, although after tonight, he would have to find a new place to hide out.

That familiar tingle started inside him.

He loved that rush he got when he stole another person's life. Something that wasn't his to take, but that just made it all the sweeter.

Parking the car, he strode into the cabin. "Honey, I'm home," he called out, the same thing he had said to Meadow every night when he returned home. Only then there would be a hot meal waiting on the table, a bath drawn and ready for him after he ate, and Meadow dressed in the outfit he had chosen for her that morning ready to offer her body to him for whatever purpose he chose.

This was different, there was no meal and no bath, but the girl he'd abducted jogging at the park was certainly waiting for him, her body ready for him to do with as he pleased. When he'd left to follow Meadow, he'd left the girl with a noose around her neck balanced precariously on her tiptoes, and he had been wondering the whole drive back whether she would still be alive when he returned.

From the way her body jerked at his voice, he knew she was still alive.

Perfect because he was looking forward to slitting her open and watching her blood flood from her body taking her life along with it.

"Miss me?" he asked, standing in front of the girl.

She trembled, and her terrified eyes were fixed firmly on the floor. She was gagged so she couldn't give a verbal answer, but she refrained from a non-verbal one as well, having already learned there was no good answer to give when he asked a question.

Her fear spurring him on, he walked over to the desk where he had left his knife. This knife was special to him, he'd bought it when he was wooing Meadow, and he'd used it to kill every single one of his victims, including the old man he had stolen the car from yesterday. He'd also used it on Meadow more than once.

Now he took it over to where the girl was perched and pressed the blade against her neck, sliding it between her skin and the rope of the noose. Her eyes were wide and her nose flared as she dragged in a terrified breath, wondering whether he was about to slit her throat.

He wasn't.

He had a much more fun way to end her life.

Cutting through the rope, he slung the girl over his shoulder, her ankles were tied together, as were her wrists. He hadn't wanted a repeat of the whole Carla Briscoe fiasco so he'd made sure she was well and truly restrained before he'd left her alone.

Tossing her onto the bed he stood above her, enjoying his handiwork. The girl was naked, and a myriad of bruises, cuts, and bites marred her milky white flesh.

He loved that look on a woman.

Most men liked pretty dresses, sexy lingerie, or expensive

jewelry on their women, but he liked to see the marks he had put there himself.

John cut the rope binding her ankles and spread her legs. She tried to fight him, but she was a tiny little thing, no match for his strength. Kneeling between her legs he smiled at her, watching her face as he shoved the blade of the knife inside her body.

FEBRUARY 8TH

5:32 A.M.

Her naked body was warm against his, and Abe couldn't sleep because he just wanted to keep looking at her.

She was beautiful.

The more he looked at her, the more beautiful she seemed to become. Her skin was like porcelain, her nose was delicate, her limbs were long and slim, her hips had just the right amount of curve, her breasts were small but round and firm and perfect, and the swell of her stomach took a part of him he'd thought was hard as concrete and started to soften it. Her plump lips were pale and the most kissable pair of lips he had ever seen, and her voice—particularly when it was moaning his name as he worked her higher and higher and closer toward orgasm—was melodious.

She was like an angel.

If he had to pick a woman to fall for it would certainly be this smart, sweet one lying in his arms.

Meadow shifted in her sleep, her bottom brushing against him since he was spooning her, and he debated waking her up for sex before he had to go into the station. He might have, but she really did need the sleep, and he shouldn't disturb her no matter how sexy she looked tucked at his side.

Abe almost caved to the pressure when she wriggled again, but his phone rang, and he reached to grab it from the nightstand before it woke Meadow.

"What's up?" he asked quietly as he pressed answer.

"We found her," Fletcher told him.

His deputy didn't have to elaborate for him to know the *her* he was referring to. Darlene Frindlebrook's body had been found.

"Where?" he asked.

"The motel two miles east of town," Fletcher replied.

"I'll be there in twenty minutes." Abe hung up and tried to ease his arm out from underneath Meadow without waking her, but she stirred and yawned, lifting her head to look at him.

"Abe?" she asked, her voice laden with sleep.

"Shh, go back to sleep," he whispered, touching a quick kiss to her lips. He wished he had time for more, but he had work to do, and if he wanted more nights like last night with Meadow, he needed to find her husband. He'd thought he might have regrets, or feel bad, having slept with a married woman. She'd come on his tongue, on his fingers, and with him inside her twice, but he didn't feel guilt. Meadow was married in name only, that marriage had never been real, it had been just a way for John Smith to keep a victim around for whenever he wanted someone to hurt.

"Are you leaving?" she asked, waking up further and shuffling up so she was sitting.

There was no point in lying to her, this case was personal to her since she was at the center of it. "There's been another murder."

"Oh," she said softly, and he could see her curling in on herself even though she hadn't moved a millimeter. He couldn't imagine what she was feeling right now, knowing that her husband was killing people because of her, but he knew how he was feeling, and that was terror that John would get his hands on her, and a desire to wipe away all her pain and make everything better.

"Hey," he said, pulling her over so she was sitting in his lap. "I will find him, and I will make sure he pays for his crimes. And tonight I'm going to take you out for a romantic dinner, and if there's enough snow out we'll make snowmen, and snow angels, and build a snow fort, and anything else you want to do before I bring you in here and have dessert."

She shivered in his arms and shot him one of those winning smiles. "I can't wait. And be safe, Abe, please. John is dangerous, more dangerous than you know. Please don't let him hurt you, okay? I need you. We need you," she added, resting a hand on her stomach.

His hand joined hers. Being with Meadow wasn't like just dating a woman, she had a baby on the way, so being with her meant getting an instant family. For some reason that didn't scare him as much as he thought it should. "Nothing will stop me from coming home to you two, okay?"

"Ok—oh," she said her eyes flying to his. "Did you feel that?"

"I did." He grinned. "Your baby just kicked." He'd never felt that before, he hadn't even known Talia was pregnant until she had already lost the baby, and he didn't have any nieces or nephews, so he'd never been around pregnant women before now.

"That's the first time I've felt it do that. It wants you to know how important it is you come home to us too," she said seriously, although the joy at feeling her baby move still shone from her eyes.

"Meadow, you and your baby, you're my number one priority right now, I'm coming home to you," he assured her.

"Our baby," she corrected. "If you want me you get both of us."

"I want both of you," he promised, kissing her so she could feel it as well as hear the words. He wasn't ready to even contemplate the 'L' word yet, but he knew that Meadow and the baby featured quite prominently in his future.

"Good, because we want you too," she said, nuzzling his neck.

Abe groaned. "I wish I had time to make out a little, but I have to go. You should be safe here, you checked out clear when Levi looked for a tracking device yesterday, and you're not wearing the same clothes you were when you left, so there's no reason to believe that he knows you're here."

"What about my job?" she asked.

"I spoke with Maggie, she knows your situation. The job is still there for you when this is all over."

"Thank you." She leaned over and kissed him, her hands running through his hair.

"You're going to be the death of me," he groaned.

Meadow laughed. "Sorry. You're right, you should go. We'll be waiting for you when you get back."

Knowing that had never made him look forward to the end of the day more than he did right now.

Giving Meadow one last kiss, he slid her off his lap and hurried into the bathroom. By the time he had showered and dressed, he found Meadow downstairs in the kitchen, putting the lid on a plastic container.

"I made you some muesli, I hope your brother doesn't mind me going through his kitchen cupboards."

"Theo wouldn't mind at all, and thank you, you're the best. Stay inside today, call if anything seems off, I'll call to check in when I can. Be safe."

"I'll be the perfect target of a dangerous serial killer," she promised. "I won't do anything stupid, and there would be no reason John would have to check your brother's house looking for me."

"You're right, but I can't help worrying about you."

"It's mutual." She stood on tiptoes to kiss him. "Now go."

"Make yourself at home," he reminded her as he grabbed his keys and headed out the door.

Since he didn't have his car, he had to jog back to the station to use one of the patrol cars there. It didn't take long to drive the couple of miles out to the motel where Darlene Frindlebrook's body had been found. John Smith had followed through on his threat to go after residents of the town, and now that Darlene was dead Abe had to wonder who he was going to go after next.

Once they were finished at the crime scene, they were going to have to work out a plan. They couldn't just wait around while John killed more people before making a play for Meadow. Abe knew that was coming, there was no way the man could stay away from her for long. Knowing that terrified him, but right now, he didn't have a plan to stop it from happening.

The scene in the motel room was exactly what he was expecting, and yet it still took his breath away.

It was the smell of flowers.

It reminded him too much of Meadow and just how much danger she was in.

Poor Darlene's body was on the bed, battered and bruised, and slit open, her insides spilling out around her. Her breasts were missing, just like the other victims, and Abe wondered what John would do with them now that he couldn't go home.

"What's his next move?" he asked aloud. The question wasn't really directed at the crime scene techs or his deputies who were milling about, it was more thinking aloud.

"He's not planning on coming back here. This has to be where he had Carla Briscoe because there is dried blood here that's days old, so it's not Darlene's," Fletcher informed him.

"How long has he had the room rented?" Abe asked.

"The day after Meadow showed up in town," Will replied.

"So how did he know she was here?" he asked, frustrated. It was gnawing away at him, knowing that John had been able to follow Meadow here but not knowing how. If he couldn't figure out how John kept finding her, then how was he going to keep her safe?

"I don't think we're going to figure that out here," Fletcher said. "CSU will go through this place with a fine-tooth comb, and maybe they'll find something."

"Find what?" He was getting more frustrated the longer he spent here because he knew that what John had done to Darlene

Frindlebrook was exactly what he would eventually do to Meadow. Maybe not right away because she was carrying his baby, but sooner or later he would get angry enough with her that he'd kill her even if she was the mother of his child. "We know John committed the murder, we know he tortured and raped her before killing her. What we need to do is find out what he's going to do next. Until we find him, he's going to keep on killing."

Until they found him, Meadow and her baby would never be safe.

His Meadow.

Their baby.

They were his now, and he protected what was his and would do so with his dying breath if that was what it took.

John Smith was never going to touch Meadow again.

* * * * *

9:41 A.M.

Meadow hummed as she bustled about the kitchen.

Since she was stuck in the house all day until Abe came home and took her out to dinner, she was going to spend the day cooking and baking. She wanted to do something nice for Abe and his family and friends. His mother had brought her all these clothes to wear, his cousin Julian and Poppy Deveraux, who worked at the precinct as the receptionist and office manager, had stayed with her all day yesterday while Abe was working, talking to her and trying to keep her mind off her problems, and his brother Theo was letting them stay in his house.

The house smelled amazing, and her mouth was watering, she wanted to taste everything she was making, but she was making an awful lot of stuff, and she wanted to save room for wherever Abe was going to take her for dinner tonight.

She couldn't wait.

She'd never really been on real dates before.

When she was dating John, he'd taken her out for fancy dinners at the most expensive restaurants around, but now that she knew it was all just a ploy to reel her in those dates had lost their glossiness. What she had with Abe was real, it was something that she couldn't wait to see grow, and she was already daydreaming about what their future would be like.

Only this time, those daydreams were based on real feelings and not the fear that she couldn't survive on her own.

Last night had been amazing, Abe had made her feel things that she had never experienced before, and she didn't just mean sexually. He really had made her heart come alive. She'd been so overwhelmed with feelings that it had felt like her heart was going to burst.

All her life she had dreamed about being important to someone. Never knowing her father and being dumped by her mother had left her with such feelings of abandonment and inadequacy that she hadn't thought she could ever overcome them. But things with Abe were just so easy. He was letting his guard down around her, and that warmed her heart even more. His ex-fiancée had really done a number on him, cheating on him and blaming him for the miscarriage, and he'd been trying to protect his heart for so long that he'd locked it away and buried it twenty feet deep. He was digging through those layers though, and she knew that once they got to know each other better, it wouldn't be long before they were falling in love.

Pouring the last of the milk into the mixing bowl, she automatically started toward the front door, intending to take the empty carton out to the trash cans she'd seen out the front when they'd arrived there last night.

Meadow paused at the door.

She'd promised Abe that she would stay indoors all day, but surely it would be fine just to pop quickly out to the bins. It wasn't like she was leaving the property or anything, and she'd be really quick.

Yeah, it would be fine.

Still, her hand trembled as she opened the door and slipped out. It was still snowing, and a good foot or so had built up overnight. A smile lit her face as she thought about Abe's promise that they could make snowmen and snow angels tonight. She knew it was silly, but she just wanted to let her hair down and have fun. Her life had been so dark and so structured for the last five years that she just wanted to be crazy and let go.

It wasn't like she had a lot of time left to have fun.

Her baby was only four months away from making its entry into the world, and once it arrived, her world would be structured again. She would still be able to have fun, but she would then be carrying the responsibility of raising a child, caring for another human being's needs. Her baby would have to come first in everything that she did.

No, not *her* baby.

Their baby.

Hers and Abe's.

He had already promised to be there for her and the baby, and knowing that he had lost a child that was no small commitment. It was definitely a relief to know that she wasn't in this alone, and it definitely helped her to not feel so overwhelmed. It was a terrifying thing to know that she was pregnant with her abuser's baby and that both of them were in danger, but having Abe helped.

A lot.

She was a really lucky woman.

Meadow smiled and laid a hand on her stomach. She and this little guy—or girl—were truly blessed, and as nervous as she was, she also couldn't wait to meet this tiny little baby. Feeling it kick this morning had really made the pregnancy seem so much more real. It wasn't like she hadn't realized that a person was growing inside her, but she'd had bigger issues to deal with, like trying to stay alive.

But now the worst was behind her, and she and her baby could look forward to a happy future.

A normal future.

And that was all she had ever wanted. Just to be normal, to have a normal life, a family of her own, a house, a job, to worry about bills, and busy schedules, who was going to do daycare and school drop-offs, to argue about chores, and other silly things, and just to be like everyone else.

Dropping the milk carton into the trash can, she laid her hand on her stomach as she hurried back inside out of the cold.

She had only been inside for around thirty seconds when the cell phone that Abe had given her began to ring. Assuming it was Abe, a smile was already on her face when she pressed answer. "I missed you."

"Aww, well isn't that nice, I missed you too, Mrs. Smith."

Meadow almost dropped the phone.

It wasn't Abe, it was John.

How had he gotten this number?

Did he know where she was?

Quickly, she ran to the windows and closed the drapes. If he was out there she didn't want him looking in at her.

"Got nothing to say to your husband, Meadow?" John snarled.

"Wh-what? H-how? Wh-why?" she stammered.

"Cat got your tongue?" John growled. "You didn't have a problem last night letting the sheriff's tongue touch you."

She could feel the color draining from her face.

John must have been watching them.

Watching as she screamed Abe's name while he made her come with his mouth.

That meant that he knew where she was.

She wasn't safe here.

She wasn't going to be safe anywhere.

There was nothing Abe could do, there was nothing anyone

could do. Until John was dead, she was never going to be safe.

"I'm surprised at you, Meadow. Cheating on your husband, is that any way to convince a judge to give you custody of our child?"

Her heart lurched.

The cat was out of the bag now, everyone knew that John was a serial killer, he was never going to be able to go back to his job, he couldn't return to his house, he was going to prison, there was no way he could get a judge to give him custody of their baby.

She knew that and yet ... this was John.

And she wouldn't put anything past him.

"He's m-my baby," she told her husband.

"You think I'm going to let you keep him? You think I'm going to let your new sex buddy raise my child?" John's voice screamed down the phone line.

The answer to those questions was no.

She knew John would never give up his baby.

As far as he was concerned the baby was his property, just like she was, there was no way he was giving either of them up.

Not that she bothered to say that to John. He never really wanted an answer to questions he asked, he was the king of rhetorical questions, even those that didn't sound like they were rhetorical were when John was the one asking them.

"I'll never let you go, Meadow. You belong to me, and when I get you back you're going to pay for what you did. Leaving me, sleeping with that man, keeping my baby from me, and telling the cops about me so now I can't go back to my house and my job. You think that you get to play God with my life? You're wrong, I'm the God in our little universe, and when I get my hands on you I'm going to make you wish that you got off as lucky as my other victims. There's no death for you, my sweet Meadow, you're mine for the rest of your life. You're going to watch me while I play with my victims, you're going to watch while I kill them, and you're going to watch while I mold my child in my image."

The line went dead and Meadow stood there, shaking and staring at the phone in shock.

She couldn't let John get his hands on her precious little baby.

He knew where she was which meant she only had one option. She had to run.

She had to get out of here and as far away as she could before John carried through on his threat and came to get her.

* * * * *

10:03 A.M.

"CSU got samples from the victim," Fletcher told him.

"Semen?" Abe asked hopefully. Although they knew that John Smith had committed the murders, he wanted something concrete that would make sure the man would spend the rest of his life behind bars. Semen inside the victim would link him to this murder, and the specific MO with the flowers and the way he murdered his victims would link him to all the other crimes— seventeen murdered young women plus Aaron Turner. Even without the abuse of Meadow, the man would be facing several life sentences. And if they couldn't link him with forensics to the murders, the scars on Meadow's body should be enough to get him on domestic violence.

Abe wanted him to go down for all the crimes.

Meadow deserved justice for everything she had endured for five long years, and those women deserved justice too.

"Yep." Fletcher nodded, his blue eyes sparkling. "They compared it immediately to the samples we have for John Smith because they know this case is time-sensitive, and that Meadow is in danger until we get him off the streets."

"They got a match?"

"They did." Fletcher grinned.

"So we have him." Abe let out a relieved breath. He couldn't wait to tell Meadow the good news. He knew it wasn't as good as being able to tell her that her husband was off the streets and the threat hanging over her was neutralized, but at least it would give her some measure of comfort to know that they had proof of what John had done, so when they did catch him he wouldn't be getting off on any technicalities.

"We have him. Now we just need to find him."

Abe couldn't agree with his deputy more. Finding John Smith was paramount. "He didn't check in here using his real name which means he had at least one alias already prepared before Meadow left."

"He was a criminal defense lawyer, right?" Fletcher asked. When Abe nodded, he continued, "So he knew a lot of criminals, makes sense that he would have connections who could get him realistic fake IDs."

That was true, which meant that it was going to be hard to track him down. "So he has a fake ID, but he's mostly been stealing vehicles, not renting them, so I don't think he has many and he needs to save one to build a new identity with. Since he used one for this motel, but not for anything else, I don't think he has any others, which means he can't rent another room in the area. He killed Mr. Turner to get his car so I wouldn't be surprised if he doesn't kill someone else to get access to their house. We should start contacting everyone who lives on a remote property not more than an hour's drive from the middle of town because I don't think he's going to go too far away so long as he knows that Meadow is here."

"That's a good idea," Fletcher agreed. "I'm sorry, Abe, I know you've gone over this already, but I still don't know how he found her here. If he rented this room the morning after she arrived in River's End, that means he was already following her while she was on the bus because she was on the bus for two days."

"He's tracking her, it's how he knew she was here and that she was staying in my house, but we checked the clothes she was wearing when she ran, and there was nothing there. And Levi checked her out, but there were no tracking chips implanted in her."

"Jewelry?"

"No, all she had was a pair of earrings and they were clear." The more he thought about this the more frustrated he became. There had to be a tracker, it was the only way that John could have followed Meadow, but they had checked everything that he could think of and there wasn't any.

So where was it?

There was no other scenario that made sense.

There *had* to be a tracker.

It hit him all of a sudden.

The dog tags.

Her father's dog tags.

Meadow had told him that she carried them with her everywhere, and he'd seen the small box that was always in her pocket. She curled her fingers around it and held it whenever she was scared or nervous.

John had to know about it, and he had to know that it was the one thing that she would never leave behind. He couldn't put trackers in every item of clothing she owned, and if he'd put one in her she would have known about it and tried to remove it before she ran, but her father's dog tags were guaranteed to go with her no matter what.

She still had them, she'd taken them with her when they'd left his house early yesterday morning, and he'd seen them in her pocket when he'd taken her clothes off her last night when they were making out.

That meant John knew where she was right now.

"Fletch—" Abe started, but his phone rang, and he grabbed it, noticing Meadow's name on the screen. Had she seen something? Heard something? Was she calling to tell him that she had figured out John knew where she was? Not wanting to worry her if this was just a call to say hi, he forced his voice to be calm. "Hey, sunshine, what's up?"

"It's John," Meadow said, clearly panicked. "He knows where I am, he was watching us last night. He saw you with your mouth on me."

She was crying, he could hear it in her voice, he was surprised that she hadn't run the second she realized that she was in danger. "How do you know John knows where you are? How do you know he was watching us last night?"

"He called me. Abe, he called me, and he said that he's going to take the baby. I can't let him do that."

"We won't, honey, we won't let him touch your baby. Or you. It's the dog tags, your father's dog tags. That's where the tracker is; that's how he found you. I'm coming, okay? Just sit tight, make sure all the doors are locked, and wait for me. It's going to be okay, all right, baby?"

"All right." She sniffed.

"Okay," he said, regaining some control over his own emotions now that Meadow was calming down a little. "I'm on my way."

"Hurry, okay? Please. I need you," she whispered.

"On my way, sunshine, on my way," he promised.

"Can you stay on the line with me until you—" Meadow broke off as the sound of breaking glass came through the phone.

"Meadow?" he screamed, already running for the car. "What's happening?"

"John, it's John," she shrieked. There were sounds of something clunking and glass shattering, and he could hear muffled voices in the background.

"Meadow? Meadow?" he yelled, but this time there was no answer. Abe jumped into the car, threw the lights and sirens on and roared off down the road. "Meadow? I'm coming, okay? I'm coming. Just hold on. Please, hold on."

The idea that he would arrive too late almost paralyzed him.

Meadow was the first woman he had ever allowed to start breaking down the barriers he had erected around his heart. He had lost a lot of friends to bombs and guns while he was serving, and he had lost the woman he thought he had loved along with the baby he hadn't known existed.

But Meadow was a fresh start.

Something they both needed.

It was Meadow's determination not to give up, to look for the good in life, to continue searching for happiness even when it appeared that all the joy in the world had been extinguished that had made him rethink his own life choices.

Meadow really was like the sunshine.

She cleared away the darkness and the cobwebs and all the bad things and made light shine again. She had done a lot to help him change in just a couple of days, and he had already been thinking about what the future would hold. They'd go to Meadow's OB/GYN appointments together, they'd pick out nursery furniture, discuss names. He'd go to Lamaze classes with her and be there when she went into labor. He'd learn how to change diapers and get up in the night to tend to the baby so Meadow could get some rest. They'd love that baby and raise it together, and then one day maybe they might get married and add another baby to their little family.

Now it could all be over.

Meadow could be gone, and he might never get her back.

"Don't bother looking for her, Sheriff." The cold voice came down the phone he still clutched to his ear because it was like a lifeline to Meadow.

"You'll never get away with this, John," he said, just as coldly.

"Meadow is my wife, and that baby she's carrying is my child, and I don't appreciate another man stepping in and trying to mark his territory. You're lucky I don't have a lot of time otherwise I'd gut you like a fish before I leave with my wife and baby. Actually, maybe this way is better. This way you get to spend the rest of your life knowing that she's with me. You know what I'll be doing to her because you've already seen my work. Enjoy your day, Sheriff, have fun dealing with my little going away gift." John laughed and then the line went dead.

Darlene had been a distraction. John had known where they were, and he'd known that they wouldn't have suspected that he knew where Meadow was staying, so all he'd had to do was plant a distraction and wait for them all to go running off, leaving Meadow alone and vulnerable.

And he'd fallen for it.

He had played right into John's hands, and now Meadow was paying the price.

* * * * *

10:19 A.M.

Pure unadulterated terror washed over her.

It was over.

She was right back where she had started, only this time she was in a much worse position than she had been in before she left.

Now she had made John angry, and she could tell he couldn't wait to get her alone so he could punish her.

It would be bad.

Maybe the fact that she was pregnant would make him ease up a little, but when he was like this his anger consumed him, and he couldn't always make sensible choices.

"You try anything stupid, and I shoot anyone and everyone I see, and then once I have you locked away someplace I'll come back, and I'll skin that sheriff of yours alive," John told her. "We walk out of here, straight to my car. You keep your mouth shut and no one will get hurt, understand?"

Meadow wanted to disagree, she wanted to tell him that she

was different now, that she knew what it was like to be free and she would never stop fighting him because she didn't want to give up this feeling.

But what choice did she have?

There was no way she would risk innocent people's lives, and there was definitely no way she would risk Abe's life.

So she would have to go with John and pray that Abe could find a way to find her.

"I understand," she said softly.

"There's my good girl." John patted her head like she was his dog and not his wife and then shoved a gun into her ribs, a reminder that if she didn't go along with him he would start shooting.

He led her out of Abe's brother's house, down the path, and over to a car parked a couple of houses down the street.

"You drive," he hissed in her ear, "but get in the passenger side and move across into the driver's seat."

Too afraid not to, Meadow did as she was told. There was no point in fighting it. What good did that ever do? All her life she had been fighting what fate seemed to be insisting was her life. She kept looking for more, she kept looking for love and a place to belong, but no matter how hard she searched, or how close she thought she had come to finding it, fate always tore it away from her.

Climbing up into the truck, she shimmied sideways and into the driver's seat, and as soon as he was sitting beside her, John shoved the gun back into her ribs.

"You follow my directions and no one else has to get hurt," he reminded her. "Now, drive straight down to the end of this street and turn left."

Meadow turned the engine on and began to drive. She was halfway down the block when she saw a cruiser come flying down the street, lights flashing and sirens screaming.

It was Abe.

He had been so close.

Just minutes away from saving her.

But minutes might as well be years when it meant that he was too late.

They drove past him, and as they did, Meadow felt her stomach drop. It really was over, any hope that Abe might arrive in time to save her was gone, and now she was on her own.

On her own with a monster.

They drove in silence, John barking out commands about when and where she should make a turn, but other than that the only thing that filled the car was stifling fear.

Her fear.

John was his usual ball of tightly wound up anger, and she knew that he was just waiting until they got wherever they were going before he unleashed it on her.

As they drove, she wondered where they were going.

She knew they couldn't go back to their house—which was really John's house that he had moved her into after their marriage—because the cops were on to him. Had he bought another house? Were they going to keep driving for days getting further and further away from Abe?

No.

She didn't think that he could last that long.

She had betrayed him by leaving and taking his unborn baby along with her, and she knew that he was itching to punish her for that.

He would be planning to stop somewhere fairly close by, probably spend a couple of days there while he let out his pent up anger, and then he would take her on to wherever he had decided was a safe place to stay.

That meant that Abe had a couple of days, tops to find her.

Could he do that?

She prayed that he could, but she didn't want to get her hopes up too high. Meadow knew that she had to prepare herself for the possibility that she would never again escape from John's clutches. This could be her life now so she had to find a way to be strong because in just a few months her baby would be born, and there was no way she was letting her husband turn their child into a monster.

No way.

Wasn't going to happen.

Not so long as she was alive to stop it anyway.

And just how long she would remain alive was still up for grabs.

"Next right, and at the end of the street is the house I've procured for us to spend the next little while in."

She didn't even want to know what he meant by procured, she had a sinking feeling that she already knew. If she had to guess, he probably killed whoever lived in the house.

Now it all seemed so obvious. How hadn't she known that John was a serial killer?

As they neared their destination, Meadow slowed down, she knew it was only delaying the inevitable, but she needed these last few minutes to gather herself. She knew that Abe was going to be looking for her, all she had to do was hold on, endure whatever John threw at her, and stay alive long enough for him to come for her.

He would come.

He would.

Abe would never rest until he found her.

A sad smile curved her lips up. She had finally found a good guy, one who wanted to be with her so much that he was willing to help raise her baby, and her husband had to ruin it.

Still, at least she'd had these last couple of days. She'd been held in strong arms, cradled against a hard chest, kissed and touched, comforted as she cried, made to feel safe, and most importantly made to feel loved.

They hadn't said the words, they both knew it was too soon,

but that didn't change the fact that she knew that it was coming.

Those feelings were already there, they just needed time to be nurtured and grow.

Those feelings, what Abe had given her, she was going to have to cherish those moments, hold on to them, let them keep her going when she felt like giving up. Because no matter where John took her, or how much time passed, Abe would never give up on her, so she couldn't give up on him either.

"I have a gift for you," John told her when she finally parked the car outside a pretty white farmhouse in the middle of the forest. There was no one around to hear her screams, no one around to help her, no one except her and John.

"Wh-what is it?" she asked, sure she didn't want to know.

"I'll give it to you once we get inside," he told her, keeping the gun on her as he climbed out of the truck.

Knowing that she didn't have a choice, if she tried to run John wouldn't hesitate to shoot her, she walked ahead of him into the house.

"Upstairs to the bedroom, I don't trust you anymore, little wifey." He grinned at her.

Meadow traipsed up the stairs, and he directed her into a bedroom with a large four-poster bed. She knew what was going to happen next even before he said the words.

"Strip," John ordered.

She could fight it, but what would be the point?

With a deep, resigned sigh, Meadow removed her socks and shoes, her pink sweater and jeans, then her bra and panties. She felt so exposed, standing naked before him. He was her husband so obviously he had seen her naked before, but this was different. Since she and Abe had been together she now felt like her body belonged to him and not to John.

With her naked, she had expected him to order her to the bed, but instead he slammed the butt of the gun into her chest.

Once.

Twice.

Three times.

Four times.

And then once more.

Pain splintered through her. She was sure he had cracked some ribs, she'd crumpled to the carpeted floor after the third blow, and he stood above her. His heavy boot stomped on one of her wrists, and then he put his other boot on her other wrist, pinning her to the floor.

He leaned down and gave her a box wrapped with brightly colored ribbon. "Here's your gift." He beamed.

Since she couldn't open it with his shoes trapping her wrists, he opened it for her and then lifted the lid so she could see inside.

Inside the box laid four lumps of flesh.

Four lumps of flesh with nipples on them.

These were the breasts of his last two victims.

She was gasping for each puff of air she inhaled, the bones in her wrists felt like they were going to be crushed at any second, pain engulfed her entire body, and seeing what he had done to those poor innocent women was the final straw that broke the camel's back.

Meadow turned her head to the side and threw up.

* * * * *

10:22 A.M.

Abe had never been this scared in his life.

He had fought in a war, he had been under heavy fire, he had been in explosions, he had seen friends—who were more like brothers to him—dead and dying, but there was nothing like knowing someone you cared deeply about was in trouble, and you couldn't help her.

Tires screeching, he pulled to a stop outside Theo's house and jumped out. The first thing he noticed was that the front door was wide open.

He knew what that meant.

He was too late.

They were already gone.

Still, that tiny glimmer of hope was there as he ran inside, there was shattered glass on the floor, and a chair had been knocked over. The kitchen counters were covered in various dishes and plates of cookies, and a pie was lying on the kitchen floor, pieces of crust and apple strewn around it, and the phone he had bought for Meadow lay on the ground.

It had been smashed.

Abe took in the scene. It was a pretty typical kidnapping scene, but what gave him hope was the fact that the chair was knocked over, that the pie looked like it had been thrown, those were signs of a scuffle, and as much as they terrified him because it meant Meadow had been kidnapped it also reassured him because she had fought back.

She had fought back.

That made all the difference.

If Meadow was going to stand a chance at surviving this then she had to stay strong, and if she had fought for her life against a man he knew terrified her then it meant that she hadn't given up.

"Please, Meadow, don't give up," he muttered under his breath. "I'm coming for you, I won't ever give up on you. Ever. So don't you dare give up on me."

He would do whatever it took to find Meadow, he would spend the rest of his life looking for her, he would go to the end of the earth, he would search every corner of the world, he would never give up. Meadow needed him and he had promised her that he would be there for her and the baby—*their* baby—and he intended to keep that promise.

"We'll get her back."

The words and the sudden presence beside him startled him

out of his thoughts, and he turned to see Will standing there. He knew that by now everyone in the town knew that he and Meadow were involved so there was no point in pretending that they weren't. This case was personal to him, way more personal than he'd have thought given that he had only known Meadow for a few days, but it was what it was, and he *did* have feelings for her, so he had to eat, sleep, and breathe this case until he had Meadow back in his arms.

"CSU is coming, they'll go over this place, and if he left anything behind we'll find it," Will promised.

"He won't have left anything behind," he contradicted. John Smith was too smart to make rookie mistakes, he'd been doing this for a long time, and if Meadow hadn't found the courage to run for her life they would never have known that John was a serial killer.

"I wouldn't be so sure about that," Will said. "He's already slipping, he's starting to make mistakes, his perfectly constructed world is falling apart. His secret is out, everyone knows now that he's a serial killer and that he's been abusing his wife. His wife ran, meaning he doesn't have the control over her that he thought he did, and that would hurt. And not only did she leave but she took his baby along with her. In his mind they're both his, and that would have made him angry. He's distracted and that's making him sloppy, he left behind semen at the last crime scene, and he used up his spare fake ID at the motel so now he's stuck having to find someplace to hide out. I wouldn't be surprised if he made more mistakes."

That was true.

And it was reassuring.

He had to keep holding onto that. John was slipping, and it was leading him to make mistakes that he hadn't in the past, but that also meant that as he devolved and got more careless, he was more likely to take bigger risks, and that might not work in Meadow's favor.

That John was going to hurt Meadow was a given, there was no use pretending it wasn't going to happen, the best he could hope for was that Meadow's pregnancy might mean he showed a measure of restraint when he punished her for leaving him.

"All right," he nodded his agreement, "it's a possibility that he messed up and left something behind, but I don't want us to put all our eggs in that basket."

"You want us to keep contacting all remote properties around River's End in case he's holed up at one of them?" Will asked.

"Yes." Abe didn't like the idea that he was actually praying that John Smith had ambushed one of the families that were his responsibility to care for, no doubt killing them just so that he could hide out in their house, but if John hadn't chosen to stay nearby then the chances of him finding Meadow were slim.

He also didn't like the idea of having to sit back and play a game of chance.

He wanted something concrete to do.

Careful to avoid touching anything, Abe began to walk through the open plan living room, looking for anything that could be a clue.

Something flashed and drew his attention, and stooping down he saw that it was the dog tags. Meadow must have dropped them when John took her. Slipping on a latex glove, he picked them up.

"Is that the dog tags?" Will asked, coming up beside him. "Fletcher said that's how he tracked her."

"He used something that was so special to her against her," he said, holding on to the tags and praying it wasn't all he ended up with. A few special moments and some dog tags didn't seem like enough when he had imagined them having so much more.

Having everything.

Before Meadow, he hadn't thought he'd ever want the whole marriage, wife, family thing, but now he knew he did.

"These were the only thing she had from her father. He was killed in action, after that her mother gave her up, all she wanted was someone to love her, she wanted to find her place in the world."

"And she found it with you," his cousin reminded him.

That might be true, but he wished he had given her so much more. If he could have, he would give her everything in the world, he would give her enough to make up for everything that she had missed out on as a child growing up in foster care, and everything that John Smith had put her through which was about as far away from what marriage was about as it was possible to be.

"It was the fact that she was vulnerable that no doubt attracted John to Meadow in the first place," Will said thoughtfully.

Turning to look at his deputy, he asked, "So?"

"So I bet that if we went through all the other victims we would find that they were all vulnerable as well. They came from broken homes, grew up in foster care, lost a parent at a young age, went through something traumatic. It's what turns him on, it's what he looks for in a woman because he knows he'll be able to lure them in without any trouble."

"And?" he prompted. Why was his cousin just repeating everything they already knew? They knew John had targeted Meadow because of her past and its effect on her, and it stood to reason he had chosen his other victims the same way. Abe just didn't see how that helped them right now.

"He's off-script right now, he doesn't have the time to spend working on his next victim, but some things are ingrained in him, I think if you're right and he is looking to find a house where he can hole up for a few days, then he's going to try to find someone he could sweet talk into letting him in. We should be looking for any houses where a single woman lives alone, and one who is a little vulnerable."

That actually made sense.

All John would have to do is go up to the door with a semi-believable story and feel the woman out. Someone who had spent as much time weeding through thousands of young women to find the ones who would be susceptible to his ploys should easily be able to find it in a potential victim the second he saw them.

If Will was right, they should have just dramatically cut the number of houses they had to search, and dramatically increased the chances of them finding Meadow before that man had a chance to hurt her again.

* * * * *

12:12 P.M.

Everything was falling back into place.

His wife and his child were back with him, John had new identities for them all lined up and ready to go, they'd stay here for a few days while he regained his control by teaching Meadow a lesson, and then he'd use the car of the woman whose house he was in right now to drive them out of this town. He'd dump the car after a day or so, once he was far enough away from River's End, then he'd buy a new car, and they would drive on till they got to the house he had prepared for them.

It was all going to work out.

Sure, it was an inconvenience to have to leave his life behind and start from scratch, and it would take time to build up the kind of life he was accustomed to living, but he was confident that he could do it.

All that really mattered was that he had Meadow back.

She was waiting for him upstairs, tied to the bed. He'd hit her several times, he probably shouldn't have been quite so vicious about it, but he was angry, and he wanted her to know it. *No one* bested him and got away with it. Not in the courtroom—which was why he had a one hundred percent success rate at getting his clients off—and not in his personal life either.

He would have to show more restraint when it came to Meadow, he didn't want to do anything to cause her to go into premature labor and lose the baby, so hitting her again wasn't a good idea. Not that that mattered, he had something else in mind for his beautiful wife.

With a smile on his face, he threw the body of the woman who owned the house into the shallow grave he had just finished digging then dropped a few shovelfuls of dirt on top of it. Satisfied that the body was well enough hidden that should anyone come around they wouldn't notice it, he threw the shovel into the garage and headed back upstairs.

"Honey, I'm home," he called out as he walked into the bedroom. He knew Meadow hated it when he announced himself like that when he would arrive home from work. He supposed it was because calling her honey implied a level of intimacy and care that they didn't have; terms of endearment didn't usually come from the person who made your life a living hell.

As his wife's terrified blue eyes darted to the door, he realized just how much he enjoyed tormenting her.

He really was an evil monster.

"John, please," she rasped. Her face was shadowed with pain, and she flinched with each breath she took. "Please don't hurt me again. The baby, I'm scared, I don't want anything to happen to it."

This was new.

Meadow never usually begged him to leave her alone, she usually just stood there and let him do whatever he wanted to her.

This was definitely more fun.

"Do you think I would do anything to hurt *my* baby?" he asked, walking over to the bed and standing beside her.

She shrunk away from him, and her eyes couldn't quite meet his, but she said, "Abe told me about your mom. He said that your mom is in a psychiatric hospital because she became catatonic after she was charged with sexually abusing you, but ..." she trailed off but chanced a quick look at him. "But he thought that maybe you lied about that. Did you?"

Why all of a sudden was she so interested in his past?

They had been married for five years, but they had never really talked much about him. There had been no need to, his past and who he was had nothing to do with their relationship.

"So full of questions, my sweet Meadow," he said, running his fingers through her blonde locks. She trembled beneath his touch, and he relished the knowledge that he was so much bigger than her, he could crush her if he wanted to. Her diminutive size and fragility were what had attracted him to her in the first place, he liked to prey on women who were much smaller than him. Pick on someone your own size was not a principle he had ever taken too seriously.

"You did lie, didn't you?" she asked, her expression pained like she kept learning more and more horrible things about him.

"What does it matter?" he asked as he sat beside her on the bed. "Do you really care whether or not I lied about my mother abusing me?"

"I do," she whispered. "You're the father of my baby, I want to know everything about you. You owe me that." She eyed him defiantly. "You tricked me into marriage and now I'm pregnant, tell me everything about you. Please." Her voice wobbled on that last word, but her gaze didn't waver.

"My little Meadow is growing up." He grinned down at her, tracing his fingertips up and down her bare stomach. She sucked in a breath at his touch and winced at the movement. A mass of goose pimples broke out on her flesh, John knew they were from fear, not arousal. "Okay, you want to know everything, fine. My mother never laid a hand on me. After my father left she was so pathetic, whining and crying, she was such a sniveling little mess, and I got tired of her, I wanted her out of the house, I wanted to be free to live my own life. With her out of the way I went into foster care, and well, you know what that's like." He paused to smile at her, trailing his finger up to touch one of her breasts. "No one cares about you, no one loves you, you're nothing, a no one, and that meant I could be anyone I wanted."

"A murderer," she murmured.

"Not at first," he mused. "At first I just enjoyed the freedom of being alone, I relished it. I loved my job, I loved getting criminals off, and I loved what I learned from each and every one of them. Then I wanted more, and well, I think you know the rest."

Meadow was breathing hard, tears snaked down her pale cheeks and the sight of them turned him on like nothing else could. His wife wanted some sort of answers as to why he was the way he was, like that would somehow make everything make sense, and that would make it better.

But there was no answer to why he was the way he was.

He hadn't been abused, his father may have left, but the man had simply moved on, he hadn't been a bad man. His mother, while a pathetic mess wasn't a bad woman, she had just annoyed him, and he'd wanted an easy out. There was no trauma, no drug or alcohol abuse in his past, there was no head injury, there was no disease, his brain was simply wired to enjoy another's pain.

"Stop looking for answers, Meadow, there aren't any. This is me, and I'm the man you chose to marry, although I see you haven't been taking those vows too seriously. Letting that man touch you."

His light grip on her breast tightened. John watched the expression on her face, it morphed from discomfort, to pain, to agony, as he crushed it with a bruising strength.

It wasn't enough.

He needed more.

He wanted her to suffer, make her feel what he had felt watching another man touch his wife.

Meadow's naked form was secured to the bed, her wrists and ankles tied to the bedposts, and he liked her this way. Spread open and completely vulnerable to him.

John stood and let his hands wander his wife's body. It was

almost like seeing it for the first time. His Meadow wasn't quite the woman he thought she was. She was stronger than he had given her credit for, and cracking and splintering her into a million pieces which he would then reassemble in the model of his choosing was going to be fun.

His hand settled between her legs and he touched her, relishing the resigned fear on her face.

"Hmm," he drawled as he stroked her, "when your boyfriend was touching you, you seemed to enjoy his mouth on you. Maybe we should start there." John winked at her as he moved to the end of the bed and settled between her legs.

Her strangled sob when his mouth touched her soothed his soul.

He didn't feel guilt.

He didn't feel remorse.

He didn't mind torturing his own wife.

He didn't mind molding his own child into his image.

He didn't mind killing and maiming innocent young women.

He was the perfect killing machine, he was smarter and more cunning than any criminal he had ever defended, and he enjoyed this, his wife's squirms and little moans of torment at the ministrations of his tongue turned him on like nothing else could, and he was glad he had the entire rest of his life to make her suffer for thinking that she could leave him.

* * * * *

4:31 P.M.

Too much time had passed.

It had been over six hours since John had kidnapped Meadow. That was more than enough time for him to have done whatever he wanted to her.

The thought of her in pain sliced at his heart.

For so long Abe had thought he'd stamped out any lingering desire to fall in love and have a family of his own one day. Loving someone meant leaving yourself open for crushing pain.

He had loved Talia.

Deeply and truly.

He had believed that she'd felt the same way, but he couldn't have been more wrong. It wasn't that she hadn't loved him that had hurt, it wasn't even that she had cheated on him while he was off overseas fighting to keep their country safe. It was that she had kept the fact that she was pregnant a secret and then used the miscarriage as a weapon against him, a way to justify her cheating.

That was what had cut so deeply at his heart that he had decided he would rather be alone than give another person the ability to hurt him like that again.

What was the point of falling in love when all you got was a broken heart?

He would have loved to be a dad, and he would have done everything within his power to make sure that his son or daughter had the happiest life possible. He would have emailed or video chatted every day that he could while he was on tour, and when he was home, his child would have gotten his full attention. They would have gone camping, played trains or dolls or whatever his child was interested in, he'd coach their sports team, and go to parent-teacher conferences, and he'd make sure that his child knew that they could come to him with any problem, no matter how old they got.

The loss of that baby still hurt, and he hadn't even known it existed until years after it was gone.

But everything had changed since he met Meadow.

She was the opposite of Talia. His ex-fiancée had been spoiled, used to getting her own way and throwing a temper tantrum when she didn't get it. She was popular and was the girl who all the girls wanted to be, and all the boys wanted to sleep with. Back then, it had stoked his ego that the sexiest girl in the school wanted him, and he had taken every opportunity to throw that in his friends' faces.

Now he knew that looks and heart were two different things.

Talia hadn't loved him, he wasn't even sure that she had been capable of loving another person back then, she had been too self-centered, conceited, and self-involved. Their relationship had been doomed from the beginning, but sometimes it took time and perspective to realize that. Things with Talia hadn't ended because allowing someone to own your heart meant that they would hurt you, but because he and Talia just weren't suited. He wanted more from a wife than someone who was good in bed, gorgeous, and who wouldn't step out of the house without their hair, makeup, and outfit perfect. He wanted someone who cared about him and his needs, who wanted to stand beside him when things were tough as well as when everything was going smoothly. He wanted a partner, he wanted someone with a good heart, he wanted someone who knew that the exterior of a person wasn't as important as what was underneath.

He wanted someone like Meadow.

And he'd had her.

Her declaration that when she had cooked that meal for him back at his cabin she had been trying to convince him to like her because she felt like she needed someone to look after her was what had convinced him that this was different. She had been honest with him, and she'd admitted that she had done something wrong, and then her sweet pronouncement that now her feelings were real had made that wall around his heart start to crumble.

Honesty could be hard sometimes, but Meadow hadn't shied away from it. She had told him everything about herself, even the things that worried her like her concerns that her desire to chase after happiness rather than hide in a corner meant there was something wrong with her.

Abe didn't see things that way.

He saw Meadow as an inspiration.

If she could grow up knowing she was unwanted, without a family and support system, then spend years in an abusive marriage and still want to run after an opportunity at happiness then why should he sulk away, licking his wounds over a broken heart?

There was still a lot about each other that he and Meadow needed to learn, and they still had to see if they were compatible in terms of a relationship, but as far as he was concerned all of those things were just a formality. He already knew that they were compatible, and he was excited to learn more about the real Meadow and not just the one she had been forced to become to survive her husband's abuse.

He looked up as the door to his office swung open. He had retreated in there because he needed to be alone, he couldn't keep his fears under control and function as the sheriff at the same time. So he was hiding out in there, alone, barely holding on to his emotions, and only doing so because Meadow needed him.

"Do you have something?" he demanded, more harshly than he should have. It wasn't his deputy's fault that John had gotten to Meadow.

It was his.

He should have known that it was the dog tags. Looking back, what else could it be? It had to be something that John would know Meadow could never live without, and he was sure Meadow didn't own a single other thing that she cared about besides those tags. It was all so obvious, and if he had just figured it out earlier then he would have taken the dog tags from her, locked her away someplace safe, and used her father's dog tags as a trap to catch her husband.

Instead, he had left Meadow alone, and John had gotten her back.

Meadow was paying the price for that mistake, and that made him want to rip out his own heart because it was hurting too badly.

"Maybe," Will said, hedging his bets both ways as he came into the office and took a seat on the other side of the desk.

"Well, spit it out," he growled. This was hell, and he needed to get Meadow back before he lost his mind.

"Since we don't have enough of us to go out to every house surrounding River's End, we're having to call residents to account for them."

"I know that already," he snapped.

Will nodded patiently before continuing, "If we thought that the resident fitted our profile of a single woman living alone who might have a vulnerability that John Smith could exploit and they weren't answering our calls, then we'd head out to their house and check it out, and we think we've found someone."

"Who?"

"Taralynn Roberts. She's recently widowed, her husband had fought a long battle with cancer, finally succumbing to it about six months ago. At the funeral, she found out that her husband had been cheating on her for most of their marriage and that the woman he'd been having an affair with had had a child with him. She hadn't been able to have children, and the blow of losing the man she loved and then learning just what kind of man he was after he was already gone and she couldn't confront him about it kind of had her withdrawing from family and friends. She hardly ever leaves her house these days, she doesn't really talk to anyone, so if John had killed her so he can hide out at her house, then it would likely be days before anyone noticed. She lives on ten acres of forest about twenty miles west of town, it's secluded, her nearest neighbor is over a mile away, it's just the kind of place that John would be looking for. I've tried calling and texting in case she doesn't like talking to people and ignores phone calls, and she hasn't answered."

"Let's go," he said, already standing and grabbing his jacket and keys.

"They might not be there," Will warned.

"And that's why Fletcher and Julian will continue to contact anyone else who fits our profile while we go and check it out," Abe said, practically running out the door. The Roberts house was a little over twenty miles away from the police station, it had been snowing overnight, and although it had stopped now it was still slick out, so even with lights and sirens going it would take at least fifteen minutes, maybe more, to get out there.

That was fifteen minutes Meadow might not have.

Just because he believed that John Smith wanted his baby enough not to kill her, didn't mean he wouldn't get carried away and accidentally kill her.

Even if he didn't he would be hurting her.

And that was enough to shred him inside.

Meadow had been through so much, and she deserved to feel safe and finally be at peace. When he found her, he was going to make sure she never suffered again.

* * * * *

4:40 P.M.

Her whole body burned with pain.

Inside and out.

Meadow felt woozy, lightheaded, and that scared her. She had to have her wits about her if she was going to find a way to escape. Her chest ached with each shallow breath that she took, and her head beat with a steady drumming of pain from him hitting her. Her insides felt like they had been ripped to shreds, and there was a myriad of bruises on her arms and legs, and a particularly painful wound on her neck where he had bitten her.

The temptation to close her eyes and drift off into the sweet, peaceful blackness of oblivion was strong.

So strong she nearly gave into it.

It would be so nice to be transported out of this room, even if it was only because she had fallen into unconsciousness. There would be no more pain, no more taunting from her husband, and she wouldn't have to be reminded of the fact that she had married a heartless, vicious monster who enjoyed every second of hurting her.

Her eyes begged to close.

Surely she had put in a good enough fight so far that she deserved just a little rest.

She had confronted John, asked him about his past, she had tried her best to hold in her screams because she knew they were like music to John's ears and would only spur him on. She had fought him, maybe not physically, but she didn't know how long she would be trapped with him so the war they were fighting was a psychological one, not a physical one.

John wanted to own her soul as well as her body.

And while she couldn't stop him from owning her body, she just wasn't big and strong enough, she could stop him from owning her soul. He could only touch that if she let him. Before she hadn't had any reason to fight, she had believed John when he told her that she was nothing and couldn't survive on her own, but now she knew that was wrong. She had had a taste of true joy with Abe, and she was going to fight to get that back, even if it was just keeping those memories alive in her mind and making sure that she never forgot what Abe had taught her about herself.

She was a different person now.

One who wouldn't let John manipulate her so easily.

Meadow shifted on the bed, and a resulting stab of pain zinged its way along every single nerve ending in her body until she was engulfed in an agony that had her eyes closing no matter how much she wanted to fight.

Footsteps sounded outside the bedroom, and a moment later a shaft of light spilled over her as he must have turned on the hall light.

Instinct had Meadow evening out her breathing as best as she could and closing her eyes, trying to convince him when he came into the room that she had passed out.

John walked over to the bed. She could feel his presence beside her even though he wasn't making a sound and she hadn't opened her eyes, not even a crack.

"You think you can fight me, my sweet Meadow?" he whispered quietly, apparently fooled by her pretense at being unconscious.

Something cool and smooth touched her skin.

It was his knife.

The very knife that he had threatened to shove inside her and cut her open with if she ever betrayed him. The knife she now knew he had used to kill over a dozen innocent girls.

He pressed the blade to her cheek, then moved it so the tip scratched her flesh as he drew a line from just under her eye down to her chin. It wasn't enough to cut too deeply, but she could feel blood well up and bubble out.

She was no stranger to pain, and her body hurt enough that she didn't flinch at the new cut, instead she waited to see what John was going to do next.

"You think you can get out of this by sleeping?" he growled in her ear, so close that she could feel his hot breath against her skin. "You sleep when I give you permission, and if you think you can snatch moments of sleep then you're mistaken. Maybe I'll never let you sleep again."

John chuckled, and she felt him move away from her.

He went down to the end of the bed, and when it dipped and she felt him settle between her spread legs she wanted to scream and beg and implore him not to do that to her again. She couldn't stand the feel of him inside her. While she hadn't known just how amazing sex was when it was done right and with someone you cared about, she had always known that what John did to her was wrong on so many levels and she had always hated it so much more than the beatings. Right now, she would gladly endure whips or knives or fists or whatever else he wanted to do to her if he would just not touch her there.

Just as she felt him prodding at her entrance, she felt something lying on the pillow beside her.

The knife.

John thought that she was unconscious so he hadn't worried about leaving the knife right beside her.

Earlier, he had cut free one of the ropes he'd used to bind her limbs to the bedposts because he had wanted her to touch him.

That wrist was still free.

Her heart began to hammer in her chest.

Could she really do this?

Could she pick up that knife and kill her husband?

Anything less than killing him wasn't going to get her out of here alive, so it was all or nothing.

The idea of taking a human life made her feel ill, but what choice did she have?

Her husband was a monster, and he would never let her and their baby go as long as he was alive.

This was the only way.

John was preoccupied with readying himself to rape her, so she cautiously moved her hand until it touched the knife. Then she curled her fingers around the handle, and as John spread out above her, she lifted the knife, and her eyes popped open so she could see her target as she shoved the blade into John's neck, burying it up to the hilt.

Her husband's dark eyes grew wide, and his hands clawed at the knife, pulling it out.

That only caused the blood to flow more freely.

It squirted out, drenching John's naked body and her own.

The knife fell onto the bed beside her, and a moment later, her husband dropped to the floor.

Was he dead?

Was it over?

She hardly dared to hope that it was.

Even if he was dead she wasn't out of the woods, no one knew where she was so she couldn't just lie here and wait for the cavalry to come running to her rescue.

Picking up the knife, she tried to cut through the rope binding her other wrist. Her fingers were shaking badly, and any movement made her already aching body feel worse, but she wasn't giving up.

Taking longer than she would have liked she managed to cut through the rope on her wrist, and then the ones on her ankles.

And she was free.

Slowly, she swung her legs over the side of the bed and pushed herself into a standing position. She swayed, and her knees wanted to buckle, but she refused to let them.

She had to get out of there.

Steadfastly avoiding looking at her husband's still body, Meadow quickly grabbed the jeans and sweater she had taken off earlier and threw them on, not bothering with the underwear, she didn't have time for that. She kept expecting John to stand up at any second and launch himself at her, knocking her down and wrapping his hands around her throat, squeezing the life out of her and their baby.

Meadow couldn't find her shoes, and she didn't have time to look for them, she wanted out of there.

Now.

Grabbing the blanket that was piled on the floor on the other side of the bed, she wrapped it around herself and headed out the door.

Her legs were shaking badly, and she felt weak and drained all over, the pain made her want to give in and just curl up in a ball and let whatever happened to her happen, but she couldn't.

Every time she thought of giving up she pictured Abe's face. Those serious hazel eyes, and the red beard that she wanted to run her fingers through, the way he only quirked half his mouth up in a smile, and the way his big strong hands felt touching her body. She wanted a chance to be held in those arms of his again, she wanted to hear him call her sunshine and feel him moving inside her.

She wanted a chance at a future with him.

The only way to have that future was to get out of there.

The cold air nearly knocked her off her feet when she wrenched open the front door, but she ignored it and started running.

* * * * *

4:56 P.M.

It was exactly sixteen minutes since he and Will had left the station.

Sixteen *long* minutes as they navigated along the snow-covered roads as they drove out to Taralynn Roberts' house.

What were they going to find when they got there?

Was Meadow still alive?

Was she in one piece?

What was John going to do when he realized that he wasn't getting what he wanted?

"We should have brought more back up," Will said as Abe took a corner at breakneck speed.

"If we arrive with a whole team he's going to see us," Abe reminded his cousin. "We need to arrive silently, we don't want him to know we're there until we have the situation under control. If John knows we're there he's going to kill Meadow and the baby, he'd rather she was dead than free and someone else's."

Not just *someone* else's.

His.

Meadow was his, and he wouldn't do anything to risk her safety.

That meant that he and Will had to approach the house quietly, they would park out of sight, go the rest of the way on foot, enter the house silently and find where he was. Then once they had a clear shot of him and he was convinced that Meadow wasn't going to get caught in the crossfire, they would announce themselves. Whether he wanted to leave in handcuffs or a body bag was up to John because he wouldn't hesitate to shoot the man if he refused to surrender and presented himself as a threat to him, Will, or Meadow.

"I'm going to park here," he announced, stamping on the brakes. They were both jerked forward, but he hardly noticed the seatbelt holding him in place because he was already getting out of the car and pulling out his gun.

"I'll circle around the back, and you go in the front," Will said.

"If you see him don't shoot if he has a weapon on Meadow, I don't want her getting in the crossfire."

"Don't worry, we won't do anything to get your girl hurt."

His girl.

Abe liked the sound of that.

Meadow was his girl, and as soon as he found her he was going to make sure that she knew that. If John came peacefully, they'd get her a divorce, and if John decided he would rather go out with suicide by cop, she would be a free woman, but either way Abe knew that John Smith had never owned Meadow's heart. Their marriage had been a trap, a way to get himself a victim he had free range to do with as he pleased whenever the desire arose. As far as he was concerned, the marriage wasn't real, it had never been real, it was just a piece of paper that John had used to get what he wanted.

They split up at the tree line, and Abe dragged in a steadying breath as he prepared to cross the twenty yards or so of open space and walk inside. Never before had the stakes been so high for him personally. When he'd been serving, his team had been his family, his brothers and sisters, but this was the woman who was quickly staking a claim on his heart.

Trying not to worry about whether John was watching from a window, Abe crept across the clearing to find the front door standing wide open.

That wasn't what he had been expecting, and immediately he was on high alert.

They could have been wrong about John choosing this house, or he could have already decided that he should be moving on before he was found.

When he stepped inside the first thing that hit him was the silence.

It was quiet.

Almost too quiet.

It was like no one was there.

The possibility of finding the house empty, especially if there were signs that John had been there, was too terrifying to consider, so he shoved it away and nodded at Will as his deputy appeared on the other side of the long hallway that split the house into two.

Without exchanging a word they cleared the downstairs.

The coppery smell of blood got stronger as they headed up the stairs.

Abe counted five doors, no doubt four were bedrooms and the fifth a bathroom.

They took the one closest, and as soon as he stepped through it he froze.

Blood.

It soaked the bed, it streaked the walls, there was some on the ceiling, whoever had been in this room hadn't walked out of it alive.

Was the blood Meadow's or did it belong to Taralynn?

It made him feel like a cold-hearted monster to hope that the blood was that of thirty-eight-year-old Taralynn. The woman was innocent, she had no part in John's sick game to get his wife back, and she had already suffered a lot, that she had been tortured and murdered just so a serial killer could hide out in her house was unfair. And yet the idea that the blood was Meadow's was something he didn't even want to attempt to comprehend.

As much as he wanted answers, there were another four rooms to clear before he could find out who the blood belonged to, so he tore his gaze away from the red-streaked room and followed Will back into the hallway.

The next room they checked was empty.

As was the bathroom that came next.

That left only two rooms left.

If John was here, he could easily have heard them enter the house, he could be waiting behind the next door, a gun to Meadow's head, ready to use her as a human shield and a bargaining chip to walk out of here unharmed.

That wasn't going to happen.

There was no way Abe was surrendering Meadow to John, he'd rather die.

With Will covering him, he moved through the fourth doorway and stopped dead in his tracks.

There was a body on the floor.

A naked body.

John Smith's body.

There was a pool of blood around it, and the man's eyes were staring sightlessly at the ceiling.

There was a deep hole in his neck that looked like it had come from a knife.

The body lay beside a bed. There was a knife lying on the mattress, shorn pieces of rope lay in the four corners of the bed, blood on the pillows, and a pool of blood in the center of the mattress, right in the spot that would have been between Meadow's legs had she still been restrained there.

John had raped her.

Roughly enough to make her bleed.

He had been expecting that the man would but having that fear confirmed brought with it a surge of rage he hadn't been expecting.

Meadow was his, and he had failed to protect her from the most heinous thing that could happen to a woman.

The urge to bring John Smith back to life just so he could kill him again was strong.

"Meadow must have killed him," Will announced, crouching beside the body. The awe in his cousin's voice sparked a surge of jealousy.

"She might be hiding in here somewhere. Meadow?" he called out loudly, hoping that she was conscious so she could hear him. "Meadow? Are you here? Meadow, it's Abe, if you're here come out, or if you can't walk then call out to me and I'll come get you."

He waited for a response but there was none.

"Her clothes are gone, but her shoes are still here," Will said, standing and holding up a sneaker. "Maybe she's gone already. She had no way of knowing that we would track down where John had taken her so she might have decided her best bet was to try to find her way back into town."

Abe walked over to the window and looked out. There was snow on the ground, and the sun was already beginning to set. The Roberts' house was surrounded by forest on all sides, the nearest neighbor a mile away, if Meadow had decided to risk it and try and walk to safety she could get lost out in the forest. With the temperatures as they were and the fact that Meadow was injured, there was a very real possibility that she would never walk out of that forest alive.

Helplessness clawed at him. He'd found John Smith, he couldn't be prouder of his girl for killing her abuser and saving herself, and yet he still didn't have her safe in his arms.

No matter how hard Meadow fought to find the happiness she sought, life just wouldn't give her a break.

"I'll call search and rescue, if she was hurt she couldn't have gotten all that far, we'll find her." Will patted him on the shoulder before walking off to make the call.

He knew that the entire town would rally around Meadow, walking the forest for as long as it took to find her.

Just as he knew she could be dead by then.

* * * * *

8:36 P.M.

She had been walking for hours.

Quite possibly in circles.

When she'd left the house her mind had been fuzzy, and, not thinking clearly, she hadn't followed the road. By the time she realized her mistake and tried to backtrack to the road John had driven along she was well and truly lost.

Now she was just dragging her exhausted body through the forest, and praying she could find her way back out, because she had no idea where she was going. She might be heading toward town or further away and into the woods, she had no idea where the closest house was, or even if there were any houses close by.

It didn't help that she had a blinding headache that made just concentrating enough to put one foot in front of the other hard enough, or that her chest burned with each breath she took no matter how hard she tried to keep her breathing shallow. It didn't help that she wasn't dressed to be out in the cold and that her sweater and the blanket did little to keep her warm, or that she didn't have any shoes on so not only were her feet freezing, but the forest floor had cut them up.

She wasn't getting out of this forest alive.

That was the conclusion that Meadow had come to.

And yet despite that she couldn't stop walking.

It would be so nice to curl up at the bottom of one of the large trees, snuggle under her blanket, and just let nature take its course. She thought that hypothermia wasn't the worst way to go, in fact as far as the manner of death went it had to be one of the better ones. She would simply lie down, close her eyes, allow the darkness to tug her under, and then pass away in her sleep. It wouldn't be painful, and it wouldn't be terrifying it really would just be like sleep, only a slumber that she would never awaken from.

As tempted as she was to do just that, Meadow knew that she couldn't.

Abe would never give up on her, he would search for her for as long as it took to find her, so it felt mean to give up on him.

She couldn't do that.

She couldn't be the cause of his pain.

He had already been hurt once before by the woman he loved, and she wasn't going to do the same thing to him that Talia had done.

Even if none of this was really her fault.

She had been young and naïve when she had fallen for John's charms, and even though she was older and wiser now, it didn't undo the mistakes that she had made.

Maybe killing John made up for them.

Killing John.

That she had taken her husband's life had not sunk in yet.

It all seemed so surreal. She half expected that at any moment he would come running up behind her, or jump out from behind a tree, and grab her and punish her for stabbing him. In fact she expected it so much that she kept turning around to check the forest around her even though each movement aggravated her ribs.

"He's dead," she told herself aloud. "He can't hurt you ever again."

It was the truth, and yet she couldn't believe it.

Too many years spent living in fear of John made it hard to

believe that he was no longer a threat to her. She had been conditioned to believe that he was her god. He dictated when she was allowed to do even the most basic of things like what she ate, what she wore, when she was allowed to use the bathroom. That kind of hold wasn't easily broken, and she suspected that if she made it out of this alive that it would take a very long time to let go of that fear and level of control.

But she'd have Abe and he'd make everything better.

A smile lit her face as she thought of Abe.

He was such a good guy, she was so lucky that of all the towns she could have taken a bus to she had ended up in River's End, and of all the people who could have found her hiding behind that dumpster it was Abe Black.

She was a lucky lady.

Given the fact that she was dragging her broken and bloodied body through the forest, in the dark and cold, having just killed a man, it might seem odd to consider herself lucky, but that was how she saw things.

She had always been someone who lived for the future and what could be instead of the past or the present and what was. The past could never be changed, and the present could be endured, but the future held all kinds of possibilities, and as long as she had those possibilities then she could endure anything.

Now all those possibilities that she had dreamed about for as long as she could remember were so close she could almost touch them.

Almost.

But not quite.

Because life seemed to like to taunt her.

She could beat life at its own game though. All she had to do was find a way out of this forest, and she could have all of her dreams come true.

Meadow went to sidestep a tree—thankfully, the clouds had cleared and the moon was shining brightly, so there was enough light for her to just make out where she was going—and her bare toe rammed into the trunk.

Pain splintered through her already battered body, and a sob broke free.

She was trying so hard not to cry, stay strong, keep moving, find a way out, and get back to Abe, but it was so hard. She hurt so badly and she was so cold, and all she wanted was to be wrapped up in Abe's arms, his warm breath on the top of her head, his heart beating beneath her, his strength seeping into her.

The sobs aggravated her damaged ribs and although she tried to shove them back down tears came flooding out in a rush.

Meadow sunk down to the cold, hard ground, puddles of snow soaked through her jeans, rocks and tree roots dug into her knees, and as she wept loudly the pain in her chest became near unbearable.

She had been so close to having everything she wanted, and now it was over.

It was all over.

She was going to die out here.

Alone.

Just like she had spent most of her life.

Well, not completely alone.

Meadow pressed a hand to her stomach. Her baby was what had given her the courage to run. It was one thing to allow herself to remain John's prisoner because she was scared and beaten down until she no longer believed in herself, but it was quite another to allow him to put a hand on her baby.

That she couldn't allow.

So she had done the right thing.

She had tried to protect this little baby growing inside of her only she hadn't.

Despite her very best efforts, she had failed and now they were both going to die.

"No," she tried to rouse herself. "No."

She couldn't give up on this baby, on Abe, or on herself.

Somehow she managed to push back up to her feet and staggered a few more steps before the pain got too much and she landed hard on her knees.

Her head was starting to swim.

She was so lightheaded.

Her brain begged her to stop trying and just give in, but she ignored it.

Once again she pushed up onto her feet and staggered onward.

Meadow had no idea how many times she repeated that process. She would somehow find the strength to stand, but her exhausted body couldn't make it more than a few steps before it would collapse. A short pause would give her just enough strength to stand again and get a few more steps before the inevitable collapse.

She was still crying.

The only reason she was aware of that was because the cold made her tears feel like little drops of ice sliding down her cheeks.

Her shoulder hit a tree as she stumbled too close to it and the resulting jostle to her ribs made her cry out.

This time when she hit the ground she knew she wouldn't be getting up.

She was so tired.

Too tired.

As much as she wanted to keep going, Meadow knew that she couldn't, she was physically incapable of walking any further.

Carefully she lowered herself so she was lying down. She could no longer distinguish exactly what hurt, it had all just blurred into one big mass of pain that consumed her body. She tucked the blanket over her, it didn't do a lot to keep the cold at bay, but it was better than nothing, and it did offer some comfort just to be snuggled underneath something soft and cozy.

The spot she had collapsed was right in a patch of moonlight, and as her eyes fluttered closed it was nice to feel the light on her.

It wasn't much, but if she had to die alone at least she didn't have to do it in the dark.

Her mind began to fade, and with her last little bit of strength she pictured Abe's smiling face.

"I'm sorry," she murmured. "I tried, I promise I did, I tried as hard as I could but I can't ... I can't ... sorry ..."

When she floated away, it felt like she was riding on a moonbeam up into the sky where she could be Abe's sunshine forever.

* * * * *

9:00 P.M.

"Meadow," Abe yelled as they walked through the forest.

She didn't answer him.

Whether because she wasn't close by and hadn't heard him, or because she was unconscious—or dead—and couldn't reply, he didn't know.

Everything had taken too long to get in place, as soon as he knew that Meadow had most likely gone walking off into the forest trying to find her way to safety he had wanted to get out there and start searching. But the forest was treacherous, particularly at night and when it had been snowing, and he hadn't wanted to do anything to endanger Meadow further, so he had done the right thing and waited until search and rescue had shown up.

Mia Taylor had arrived with her entire team. They'd quickly divided the search area up into grids, based on the maximum amount of time Meadow might have been out there and how far she could go in a best-case scenario. They had assigned a grid to each team, and now they had been out traipsing through the forest for the last couple of hours.

So far there had been no sign of Meadow.

He didn't want to give up on her, but it was getting harder and harder to keep hope. He knew that she was hurt, just not how badly, and he knew that she had been raped, add to that the trauma of taking a life, and he didn't think that she could have gone too far. Yet in the almost three hours they had been out here they hadn't found her.

"This takes time," Mia reminded him, obviously sensing his growing fear that they were going to find her too late. "From what you've told me about her and her inner strength and desire to survive, she's not going to give up without a fight. She killed a man to save herself for goodness sake, no sitting back and waiting for a white knight to come riding in on a white horse to save her. She's got this, you just have to believe in her."

"I'm trying," he told Mia.

Mia paused and turned to study him, in the thin light from the flashlight she wore on her head, he could see that her green eyes were full of empathy and understanding. "I know you are. But, Abe, she literally stabbed her husband in the neck to kill him, that's how much she wants to live. That drive increases the odds that we'll find her alive. Will to live plays a big part in survival, and I have never seen anyone fight that hard to live as your girl."

"She's hurt," he reminded his friend. As much as he wanted to believe Mia, and as much as he agreed that Meadow had fought hard to get free from her abusive husband, there was only so much she could do if she was injured too badly.

"Not so bad that she couldn't get out and try to find help. And from what you told us about her I think she probably has experience with being hurt and still having to get things done," Mia said gently.

Unfortunately, that was true.

Meadow wasn't new to being beaten and raped, and she no doubt still had to keep the house running to John's standards if she wanted to avoid another beating.

Since Mia was trying to encourage him and he did know that

Meadow had a drive unlike that of any other person he had ever met, Abe nodded and focused himself. Meadow was out here somewhere, waiting for him to come for her, waiting for him to fulfill his promise to her that he would be there for her, that he would protect her and keep her safe.

"Let's get going," he said.

Mia smiled at him. "We'll find her, just keep faith."

They both started walking again, turning their heads from side to side so the flashlights shed light on every inch of the forest. She could be anywhere, passed out under a tree, trying to keep warm under a bush, staggering along desperately trying to find a way out.

He'd mostly grown up in the country, he knew his way around the forest, he knew how to find his way out if he got lost, he knew how to find water and food and start a fire to keep warm, but Meadow was a city girl, he doubted she'd spent much time in the outdoors, she must be so overwhelmed trying to find an end to the seemingly endless trees.

They'd walked for maybe another five minutes when he caught sight of something.

Something pink.

It stood out amongst the browns and greens and white of the forest, and he immediately began to jog toward it.

"Mia, over here, I think I've found her," he called out as he picked up speed. "Please let it be her," he whispered to himself.

When he reached the pink blob he let out a sigh of relief.

It *was* Meadow.

She was lying huddled under a soft pink blanket, which he quickly yanked aside so he could touch his fingers to her ice-cold neck.

At first he couldn't feel a pulse and his heart lurched, but he knew enough about hypothermia to know that her pulse would be weak and could still be there even though he couldn't feel it.

"She alive?" Mia asked, leaning over, hands on her knees.

"I can't get a pulse," he replied, grabbing Meadow—who was curled in on herself—and stretching her out. He pressed one hand to her chest, the other back on her neck, and he leaned down so his cheek was just above her mouth.

There.

He felt it.

A faint puff of air against his skin.

And the hand he had on her chest was rising and falling, she was breathing, albeit shallowly.

"She's alive," he said, more to reassure himself than to inform Mia.

Mia knelt beside Meadow, a thermometer in her hand, she put it in Meadow's ear, and a moment later it beeped out a result. "Eighty-six degrees," she murmured, yanking out heat packs from her backpack. "I'm going to put these under her armpits, and them one on her chest and I want you to wrap her back up in the blanket. Keep her close to your body so your body heat can help keep her warm, and I'm going to give you another blanket to wrap around her."

"She has blood on her head," he said as he ran his hands down her body checking for any other injuries that needed to be attended to. There was bruising on her chest, and he hoped her ribs were only cracked and not broken. At her feet, he froze. They were shredded, she'd run through the forest oblivious to the damage she was doing to her bare feet, and in this moment he couldn't be more proud of her. She was something else. "And her feet are messed up." Abe gathered Meadow into his arms and paused while Mia positioned the heat packs before tucking the pink blanket, and the one Mia handed him, around her.

"She probably has a dozen other injuries, but right now, our priority is treating the hypothermia," Mia reminded him, pulling out her radio. "I'm going to tell the others we have her and that we're heading back to the Roberts house. I'll ask someone to call an ambulance so hopefully it will be there before we get there or shortly afterward so we can get her to the hospital as quickly as possible."

Thankfully Mia was so calm and in control because he certainly wasn't.

Meadow lay in his arms, her skin so pale it was translucent and tinted with blue, there was blood streaking the side of her face, there had been a bite wound on her neck, and he was sure Mia was right and there were dozens of other injuries he hadn't noticed on his quick check. She must be in pain, and when she was in pain he was in pain.

While Mia got on her radio, he clutched Meadow as closely against his chest as he could, trying to infuse her ice-cold body with his own heat.

"Meadow," he said, stroking her tangled hair. "Can you hear me? It's Abe, I'm here now, you're safe. I'm so proud of you for what you did. You didn't really need me after all, huh? You took care of him all on your own. But I'm here now, baby, so please open those beautiful eyes of yours." Meadow didn't stir, and because he needed more of a connection to her, he dipped his head and whispered his lips lightly across hers.

Like she was Sleeping Beauty at the touch of his lips, her long lashes fluttered on her white cheeks, and a moment later, he was looking down into her big, blue eyes.

Worried that she might be confused and think he was her husband, he quickly said, "It's okay, Meadow, it's Abe, not John."

For a moment she didn't say anything, and he thought she was too out of it to know what was going on, but then she looked right at him and smiled. "I know. You feel different, and your lips … I would know them anywhere. I knew you would come for me."

"Looks like you had everything under control." He knew he was grinning like an idiot but he didn't care. Meadow was awake and talking to him, she was going to be okay. John was dead, he was no longer a threat to her, and there was nothing left standing between the two of them.

"I'm so tired," she murmured, her voice weak and her eyes drooped closed.

"I know, sunshine, we're going to get you to the hospital, get you patched up, you rest now okay, I got you, you're not on your own anymore, you did your part now let me do mine and take care of you."

A small smile lit her face and then she sagged against him as she passed out. Although she was unconscious again Abe knew that she was all right and he was ready to get out of this forest.

"Let's go," Mia said briskly, slinging her backpack on.

Abe stood, Meadow in his arms, carrying her cocooned against him as he followed Mia back the way they had come. He didn't know the extent of her injuries, and she might have a road ahead of her to recover, especially psychologically, but he would be there for her every step of the way.

They were a team now.

They would face everything together.

Here on out Meadow and her baby were stuck with him.

FEBRUARY 9TH

10:50 P.M.

Very slowly, Meadow began to emerge from her little cocoon.

It was warm and dark and safe in there, and she was a little afraid that when she came out, she would have to face a reality that she wasn't quite ready for.

The first thing she noticed was that someone was holding her hand.

Abe.

Knowing that he was there beside her encouraged her that reality wouldn't be quite so bad.

Lifting her eyelids was a little harder than it should be, but when she did she was rewarded with the sight of Abe sitting at her bedside. His eyes were closed, and his head rested back against the chair, his free hand rested on his stomach and rose and fell with each breath he took.

Meadow took a moment to just watch him.

He'd come through on his promise to be there for her, and she knew that every promise he had made to her he would fulfill. He was such a good guy and she was so glad that they still had a chance to have the future they had talked about.

The future she had been dreaming of since she was a little girl.

She shifted slightly on the bed and immediately realized what a mistake moving had been. All the pain that had been hidden because she was still partially stuck in her little bubble reared its ugly head.

She groaned, and Abe immediately snapped to attention.

"You're awake." He grinned and stood up, leaning down to touch a kiss to her forehead.

"Yeah," she agreed with a grimace.

"Are you in pain?" he asked, running his fingers through her hair.

"A little," she admitted. There seemed to be no point in hiding it from him, he'd already seen what she was capable of doing when she was backed into a corner so she didn't feel like she had to put on a strong front right now.

"I'll go grab a doctor and ask them to give you more pain relief," he said, tapping the back of her hand where a needle was connected to an IV bag hanging behind her bed.

"No, don't go," she begged, reaching for his hand. She didn't want to be alone right now. "Please, stay with me."

"All right," he agreed, perching on the edge of the bed. "I'm so glad you're awake, you scared me to death, sunshine."

"Sorry." Meadow hated the fact that Abe had been worried about her, in abducting her John hadn't just hurt her but Abe too, and that upset her more than what he had done to her. "How long was I out?"

"We found you around nine-thirty last night, it's now nearly eleven at night, so you've been out a little over twenty-four hours."

"Wow." She hadn't realized she had been unconscious for so long. While she knew John had hurt her badly, she had no idea just how badly.

"You were a little banged up." Abe smiled, but the fear was still there in his eyes. He took her hand and laced their fingers together. "But doctors say you're going to be fine with time and a lot of rest."

"What did he do to me?"

"I don't think you need the details right now," he told her.

Right now she did need details, she needed information, had to know what she was dealing with. The more she was awake the more she was leaving her little bubble, and to survive outside it she needed to be armed with every piece of information she could get. "Please, Abe, I know it might not make sense to you, but I need to know. I know he hit me, and I know he bit me a few times, but I want to know."

Abe sighed and looked like he strongly disagreed with this, but then he said, "You have three cracked ribs, a concussion, there were four deep bites where he broke the skin, bruises everywhere, since you didn't have your shoes on when you ran your feet got cut up pretty badly, and there was some internal damage from him, uh, raping you." Abe seemed to struggle to get the word out. "I don't know how you managed to walk for miles through the forest. Well, actually I do because you're amazing." He brushed the back of his knuckles across her cheek.

His report of her injuries wasn't any worse than she had been anticipating so that was a blessing in disguise, and that Abe thought she was amazing almost made her believe that it was true. "John is really dead, right?"

"He's dead. I saw his body for myself. When I saw him, when I realized what you had done, how you had saved yourself, I have never been more proud of someone. All those things that he told you about yourself, Meadow, I hope you know that none of them are true. You are smart, and funny, and full of life, and you are more than capable of taking care of yourself and your baby without anyone's help. But ... I hope that you'll let me help. I want to be there for you, Meadow, for you and the baby. I know we haven't known each other for very long, and I know we still have a lot to learn about one another, but I really want to get to know you more, because I think we could have the future that we both want."

"Are you saying that you want us to be a couple?" She felt a little vulnerable right now, with everything that John had done, and Abe knowing about it, and she needed to hear him say the words.

"Yes, but I understand if it's too soon for you. I know that your husband only just died, and I know the hell you've been living for the last five years, plus you have a baby on the way, so if you need to go slow then that is fine. I just want you to be happy."

This *was* happening quickly.

Her husband had only just died.

She had been living in hell for the last five years.

She did have a baby on the way.

The only question was whether or not she wanted to take things slowly.

Meadow had a lot of regrets. She regretted that she had been so naïve and starved for love and attention that she had fallen for the first guy who had shown her even an ounce of interest. Because of that she had found herself the victim of domestic violence, she had lived with a serial killer, and she had very nearly gotten herself killed.

Was she ready to jump straight into another relationship?

Her regrets about John were never going to go away, they were a part of her now just like the psychological and physical scars that he had left her with, but she knew that Abe was nothing like John. When they had been dating, John had been all suave and charming, he'd seemed like the perfect guy, but Abe was real, he was sexy, he made her feel amazing when he touched her, he listened to her and was honest with her, he could be a little gruff, and he was rough around the edges, but he was perfect.

He was everything she wanted.

He respected her, saw her strength and love of life, and saw her, which made him ever sexier.

Meeting Abe's gaze, she said, "I don't want to take things slow. I want us to be a couple. Like you said we still have lots to learn about each other, but I want to learn them with you as my boyfriend."

Abe relaxed, and the biggest smile she had ever seen on him spread across his face. He lifted her hand and kissed the back of it, and then turned her hand over and pressed a kiss to the inside of her wrist, making her shiver.

"No fair," she pouted, "you know I'm all banged up."

"When you get out of here I'm going to rip your clothes off and kiss every inch of this gorgeous body."

She knew he meant it to be sexy, but it reminded her that her body wasn't gorgeous, it was like a roadmap of scars.

"Your scars only make you more beautiful, they're a testament to your strength, they make you who you are," he told her, correctly interpreting her pause.

Meadow was starting to get sleepy now, but she couldn't help but smile at that. "You're almost too good to be true."

"Oh no, that's you, sunshine." Abe kissed her, and she felt that tingle start in her body, even the pain of her injuries couldn't wipe it away. "You should get some more sleep."

"Are you staying?"

"Do you really have to ask?" Abe turned around so he was stretched out on the bed beside her then carefully tugged her against him.

Meadow snuggled against his side, her body was still throbbing with pain, and her head still swum a little, there was a coldness in her bones that she suspected might hang around for a while, and she felt like she could sleep for a month, but she had never been happier in her life.

She finally had what she wanted.

A man who loved her and had pledged to be there for her, a baby who would be hers forever, a family of her own. A place she belonged.

Fighting for her happiness had finally paid off.

Content, Meadow closed her eyes and let herself drift off to sleep.

Jane has loved reading and writing since she can remember. She writes dark and disturbing crime/mystery/suspense with some romance thrown in because, well, who doesn't love romance?! She has several series including the complete Detective Parker Bell series, the Count to Ten series, the Christmas Romantic Suspense series, and the Flashes of Fate series of novelettes.

When she's not writing Jane loves to read, bake, go to the beach, ski, horse ride, and watch Disney movies. She has a black belt in Taekwondo, a 200+ collection of teddy bears, and her favorite color is pink. She has the world's two most sweet and pretty Dalmatians, Ivory and Pearl. Oh, and she also enjoys spending time with family and friends!

To connect and keep up to date please visit any of the following

Amazon – http://www.amazon.com/author/janeblythe
BookBub – https://www.bookbub.com/authors/jane-blythe
Email – mailto:janeblytheauthor@gmail.com
Facebook – http://www.facebook.com/janeblytheauthor
Goodreads – http://www.goodreads.com/author/show/6574160.Jane_Blythe
Instagram – http://www.instagram.com/jane_blythe_author
Reader Group – http://www.facebook.com/groups/janeskillersweethearts
Twitter – http://www.twitter.com/jblytheauthor
Website – http://www.janeblythe.com.au

sic enim dilexit Deus mundum ut Filium suum unigenitum daret ut omnis qui credit in eum habeat vitam aeternam

Made in the USA
Middletown, DE
23 February 2023

25479465R00137